"And What Do You Do, Mr. Durand, Besides Punch Cows?"

He looked her straight in the eye. "I'm a lawyer."

"Ah, yes, a lawyer."

"Law is generally considered an honorable profession, Miss Williams."

"There are no honorable professions, Mr. Durand. Only honorable or dishonorable men."

Nick's eyes widened appreciably as he muttered, "Good Lord, you must be a schoolteacher."

Mary Beth nearly choked on her drink. "It's worse than that, I'm afraid. I'm a librarian."

Dear Reader,

Welcome to Silhouette! Our goal is to give you hours of unbeatable reading pleasure, and we hope you'll enjoy each month's six new Silhouette Desires. These sensual, provocative love stories are both believable and compelling—sometimes they're poignant, sometimes humorous, but always enjoyable.

Indulge yourself. Experience all the passion and excitement of falling in love along with our heroine as she meets the irresistible man of her dreams and together they overcome all obstacles in the path to a happy ending.

If this is your first Desire, I hope it'll be the first of many. If you're already a Silhouette Desire reader, thanks for your support! Look for some of your favorite authors in the coming months: Stephanie James, Diana Palmer, Dixie Browning, Ann Major and Doreen Owens Malek, to name just a few.

Happy reading!

Isabel Swift
Senior Editor

SDRL-7/85

SUZANNE SIMMS
Nothing Ventured

Silhouette Desire

Published by Silhouette Books New York

America's Publisher of Contemporary Romance

SILHOUETTE BOOKS
300 E. 42nd St., New York, N.Y. 10017

Copyright © 1986 by Suzanne Guntrum

Distributed by Pocket Books

ISBN: 0-373-05258-8

First Silhouette Books printing January 1986

10 9 8 7 6 5 4 3 2 1

America's Publisher of Contemporary Romance

Printed in the U.S.A.

SUZANNE SIMMS

was born in Storm Lake, Iowa, and currently resides in Indiana with her husband and son. She has a degree in English literature, loves opera, and studied classical piano for ten years. Ms. Simms loves reading and writing romances and believes being a successful romance writer is primarily a matter of attitude.

For my big brother, Jim,
and his wife, Jan,
who introduced us to the glamour
and excitement of Las Vegas

One

The brute left her a note. He didn't even have the guts to tell her in person.

Mary Beth Williams wanted to spit.

She looked around the formal dining room of her house. The house that was going to be not *her* home, but *their* home in another four weeks. Beautifully engraved, pristine white wedding invitations were stacked everywhere. Piles of them. Piles of utterly useless pieces of paper. Jeffrey had gone. Run off. Skedaddled.

Mary Beth shook her head. There must be some mistake. It had to be someone's idea of a joke—a bad joke. She stared at the note that she clutched in her hand. It was no joke and there was no mistake about it. With its precise crossing of the *t*'s and methodical dotting of each and every *i*, the handwriting was definitely Jeffrey's. The white vellum notepaper with its letterhead printed in traditional black Roman letters was Jeffrey's. Even the rather distinctive formal style was Jeffrey Donnell through and through. She could almost imagine that he'd been tempted to begin with "We regret to inform you . . ."

All the punctilious phrases boiled down to one thing in the end: Jeffrey had run off with another woman—Joanna Whitman, to name names. Joanna Whitman, the *wife* of Dr. Osgood Whitman, one of the town's leading physicians, to be even more precise.

The man must be out of his mind, thought Mary Beth.

Her first impulse was to cry. After all, wasn't that what any woman would do if her fiancé walked out on her a month before the wedding? Her second impulse was to throw something. She fought the first impulse and won. She lost to the second.

The sheet of crumpled notepaper went flying across the dining room, and landed on a pile of neatly stacked wedding invitations at one end of the solid cherry drop leaf table. Jeffrey's letter and several invitations toppled to the carpeted floor without a sound. It was an ineffectual gesture at best, Mary Beth acknowledged as she regained control of herself. She brushed at the skirt of her classic beige shirtwaist and raised a hand to smooth her hair, but the hand she raised to her head trembled just a little all the same.

Not that her hair was mussed. It was never *really* mussed, since she preferred to wear it parted straight down the middle and pulled back from her face in a tightly anchored bun at her nape. Few women could wear that style and few women should. Mary Beth Williams was one of them.

The rather severe arrangement only served to emphasize dark, intelligent eyes and show off the prominence of her cheekbones and the aristocratic tilt to her nose. It was a hairstyle that spoke of control, propriety and an "everything-in-its-place" kind of neatness. It projected the quietly dignified image she felt was appropriate for a librarian and a Williams to boot. In short, it was the perfect style for Mary Beth.

Everything about her was dignified, understated, proper. And she thought disparagingly, no doubt bordered on the mundane as well. All five feet five inches of her were really quite ordinary, from the tips of her size seven shoes to the top of her brown-haired head.

She was essentially a *brown* sort of person. But she hadn't thought Jeffrey minded that she wasn't exciting in the way that some women were exciting. She had thought he appreciated those qualities she did possess. She'd always known that it would take a more mature, discerning male to appreciate her finer points. She wasn't flashy, glitzy or glamorous. She was calm and quiet—and deep inside, she was a romantic. And apparently something of a fool as well. She'd certainly been giving Jeffrey more credit than he was due.

Mary Beth grimaced, rubbing the sore muscles of her right hand. Drat, if the man was going to do a disappearing act, why couldn't he have done so *before* she'd addressed all those lousy invitations?

But Mary Beth Williams had been lucky, and she knew it. It could have been worse. Far worse. In another day or two the wedding invitations would have been in the mail.

Damn Jeffrey Donnell and damn his inconsiderate ways! How dare he run off and leave her holding the bag!

Wait a minute. She stopped and thought. Even a condemned man was given a last meal. She owed it to Jeffrey and herself to give him that last chance. She would call his office—although she normally frowned upon calling a man's place of business except for the most unavoidable emergencies—and she would see what he had to say for himself. Assuming he was there to say anything.

Before she could talk herself out of it, Mary Beth marched into the front hall, picked up the receiver, and dialed the number of Jeffrey R. Donnell, CPA.

She hoped and prayed for Jeffrey's sake, if not for her own, that he was in his office. How many people would trust a man with their taxes if he couldn't be trusted with their wives?

On the second ring, the telephone was answered in the distinctly businesslike voice of Miss Weintraub, sixty if she were a day and efficient as only a woman who has dedicated her life to efficiency can be. It was considered an endorsement of Jeffrey Donnell in the eyes of the community that Miss Weintraub had agreed to manage his professional life by becoming his secretary—a misnomer if there ever was one. Miss Weintraub had taken over when the young accountant opened his offices in Greensport two years ago. The rest was history.

Mary Beth had always suspected that the perfectionist in Jeffrey held some fundamental attraction for the perfectionist in Miss Josephine Weintraub. They were perfectly suited to one another, in spite of the thirty years' difference in their ages—perhaps because of it.

"Miss Weintraub, this is Mary Beth Williams," she began, observing all the necessary decorum. "May I please speak with Mr. Donnell?" Miss Weintraub wouldn't dream of referring to Jeffrey by his first name, of course. She was of the old school—although of *which* old school Mary Beth was never quite certain.

"I'm sorry, Miss Williams, but Mr. Donnell is not in his office at the moment."

"Do you know when he'll be in?" Mary Beth tried to sound as though she had a right to ask that question.

"I'm afraid I can't say, Miss Williams." Was there the slightest puzzlement, the merest hesitation in Miss Weintraub's voice? If so, it was a first. "There was a note on my desk this morning stating that Mr. Donnell had been unexpectedly called away."

Mary Beth took a fortifying breath and forced herself to ask, "Did the note say when Mr. Donnell would be back?"

"No, it didn't," the woman said, her voice matter-of-fact.

"Did it say *where* Jeffrey went?"

"No." Then silence. After a moment Miss Weintraub spoke again, in a surprisingly humane tone of voice, "If Mr. Donnell contacts the office, I could suggest that he call you, Miss Williams."

That was as much of a concession to friendship as Miss Weintraub had made in all the years Mary Beth had known her. Or perhaps, known *of* her. She didn't think anyone in Greensport really knew Josephine Weintraub. Apparently they didn't know Jeffrey Donnell as well as they'd thought either—and Mary Beth's name was at the top of *that* list!

She tried to swallow the funny little lump in her throat. "Thank you, Miss Weintraub." She set the receiver back in its cradle with deliberate care. She wanted to slam it down. All the more reason not to, of course.

"Well, Jeffrey, it looks like you've gone and done it now. But what in the world am I supposed to do?" Mary Beth heard her voice echo faintly down the long hallway that ran from the front to the back of the old Victorian-style house.

Morning sun poured in through the stained glass windows on either side of the front door, forming diamond-shaped patterns of sunlight and muted color on the marble floor in the entranceway. This part of the house was always cool, even on the hottest summer day. It was almost cold now, although it looked as though it was going to be another perfect May day outside.

Mary Beth shivered and wrapped her arms around herself. A cup of tea, that's what she needed. There was almost no problem that didn't look better over a cup of hot tea. That had been her grandmother's all-purpose solution to life—from monthly cramps to first love and its heartache to the letter telling Mary Beth of her father's remarriage only five months after her mother's death.

Have some tea, Mary Beth. You'll feel better after you have a nice cup of hot tea. She could almost hear her grandmother's voice calling to her now. If only life were that simple, Mary Beth thought, heading for the kitchen at the back of the house.

The kitchen was large and white and charmingly out-of-date. It was much as Mary Beth remembered it from her childhood, when her grandparents had lived here, and she had lived walking distance away with her parents. Years and years ago her mother had told her that it was still very much as she remembered it from her own childhood when she was the girl next door. Abigail Williams would invite her in for a cup of tea and a cookie after school.

Abigail had sons, lots of them. Four of them, in fact. But she longed for a daughter. Little wonder then that she took to the slip of a girl next door who would one day marry her youngest, and least responsible son.

Mary Beth found a certain comfort in the knowledge that this room had changed very little in the last forty years. She liked the feeling that her grandmother had stood by this sink running water for her tea kettle, and that she had sat at this table to drink her cup of tea while she looked out on the terrace and gardens below.

Mary Beth went through the ritual of preparing a pot of tea now, as if the very familiarity of the action would get her through the next minute and then the next and the next. Before she knew it an hour would be gone and then two hours and then a whole morning and finally an entire day. It seemed important, somehow, to make it through this first day. If she could face the next twenty-four hours, she could face anything.

She suddenly felt so...odd, so out of time and place. But then, who wouldn't? she thought charitably. It had been a hell of a way to find out that she was no longer engaged to be married: a letter, timed to arrive on Saturday morning. She wondered if the good doctor had received a similar note.

Her teeth sank into her lip. *Oh, Jeffrey, why?*

But she knew why. At least she knew what he'd said in his letter. She wasn't sure she really understood everything deep down in her heart. Beneath the carefully couched words and phrases, Jeffrey's meaning was clear. He wasn't ready to settle down after all—at least not with Mary Beth. To add insult to injury, he had added that the other woman in his life gave him something he never thought he'd have—excitement! She was quite capable of reading between the lines. *She* wasn't exciting.

Mary Beth stirred a spoonful of sugar into her tea, the sterling silver teaspoon clinking against the delicate bone china cup. Men were so damned unreliable! She wasn't sure she'd ever understand or trust one again. Some men would never grow up, they'd always want the thing they couldn't have—until they got it.

But Jeffrey of all people! He had always seemed so mature, so reliable. Then to go and pull an adolescent stunt like this one, and not even be man enough to tell her to her face!

Mary Beth suddenly realized how angry she was. In fact, she was furious, and she had every right to feel that way. Jeffrey could at least have had the common courtesy to tell her by a more personal means than a letter.

The coward! She could feel the scalding hot tears pricking the corners of her eyes. She wasn't one to cry, but she put her head down now and wept. She cried for love lost and the illusion of love. She cried for what might have been. She cried a little out of self-pity and a little out of anger. She cried, knowing that it would be the one and only time she would cry for Jeffrey and herself. She cried because she damned well felt like crying!

But she didn't cry for long. It was essentially a waste of time and energy. And it wreaked havoc with her face, leaving her eyes a telltale red, her complexion puffy, and her nose as pink as a rabbit's and runny. Besides, the louse wasn't worth it. Jeffrey R. Donnell, CPL: Certified Public Louse.

At that, Mary Beth laughed out loud. At least she could still laugh at Jeffrey and, even more importantly, at herself. It was something she'd had to work hard at. The Williamses weren't known for their rollicking sense of good fun. She knew all too well that she tended to take herself, and life a bit too seriously. She had assumed that Jeffrey did as well. They had been so very much alike—or so she'd thought.

Good heavens, she was already thinking of the man in the past tense. But then, Mary Beth Williams had never been one to put off a task simply because it was unpleasant. Even if it was the often difficult and unpleasant task of facing the truth. She had to face facts. She was a woman scorned. A woman left practically standing at the altar.

There were so many things that would have to be done, or rather, *undone*. Every detail she and Jeffrey had planned for the wedding ceremony and the reception following it would have to be seen to. The entire nuptial production would have to come to a screeching halt, and—like the powerful and inevitable force of a river dammed in mid-stream—not without some difficulty. She'd have to cancel the church, the caterers, the florist, the professional photographer coming all the way from Madison, the reception at the country club, the honeymoon. She'd have to notify the bridesmaids and the ushers, the minister and the organist, and the...the list was endless!

And that was only the beginning. An uncharacteristic groan of dismay slipped through Mary Beth's lips. Oh Lord, she and Jeffrey were bound to become the latest nine-day wonder in a community that thrived on nine-day wonders. They would be the subject of gossip in Greensport for weeks to come. It was all so distasteful, so... *common*.

And so unheard-of for a Williams. Unheard-of, if you didn't count her father. She'd hate that as much as anything, hearing people say "like father, like daughter." As the proverbial black sheep of the family, Gerald Williams seemed almost to enjoy his "notoriety." Mary Beth, however, was cut from different cloth. She loathed even the merest hint of scandal or gossip, regarding anything of the kind as contemptible and beneath human dignity.

She sighed resignedly and pressed her back against the sturdy kitchen chair. She might well be the innocent party in this, but people tended to blame the bride whenever anything went wrong. She knew that. There were bound to be less-than-polite stares and whispered speculations. There would, no doubt, be a thousand and one well-meaning questions. And there were going to be some long, sleepless nights ahead for her.

Mary Beth straightened her shoulders, her posture perfect, her pride intact. She would not allow Greensport to break her spirit any more than she would allow Jeffrey Donnell to break her heart. A Williams was made of sterner stuff than that, as her grandfather had been fond of saying.

At one time, the Williams family had been one of the most prominent and prosperous in the small town of Greensport, Wisconsin. Until they had fallen on hard times. It was in better times that the library had been endowed by, and named after Mary Beth's grandfather, Jonathan Horatio Williams. Jonathan Horatio Williams had been named in another age, in an age when America, at least small-town America still believed that any man could be Horatio Alger.

Unlike so many others, the Williams family failed to prosper during the war years. Mary Beth worked at the library because she needed a job to support herself. She'd always worked. She'd always had to. Despite the currently deflated financial status of her family, she was beginning to suspect that Jeffrey Donnell had all along been more intrigued with the prestige of the Williams name than with her.

Thank God, her grandfather had had the foresight to provide a trust fund to maintain the house, Mary Beth thought, as she sipped her tea and gazed around the large kitchen. She could never have afforded to live here if he hadn't, but even so, the upkeep and responsibility of the big house were sometimes more than one person could handle.

Mary Beth set the cup of hot tea down on the saucer. It was time to get down to business. She took a pad of paper and a pencil from the kitchen drawer behind her. She'd better start making that list of people and places to notify about the cancellation.

Her hand shook a little as she began to write in her neat, precise style. Then hot tears suddenly pricked her eyes once again. Oh God, to think that she'd been jilted only a few scant weeks before her wedding! How would she ever be able to live down the humiliation? She thought of locking herself in the house, or running away. In the end, they were the same, and she would do neither.

For crying out loud, Mary Beth argued with herself, she wasn't the first woman to be left stranded at the church door, and she wouldn't be the last. She had little patience or tolerance for people who went around feeling sorry for themselves. There was no room in her world for whiners.

She glanced down at the rapidly growing list beneath her fingertips. On the other hand, perhaps she had the right to whine just a little. After all, she *had* made a number of nonrefundable deposits. Damn Jeffrey! Cancelling their wedding wasn't going to cost her just her pride, but a pretty penny as well. The man wasn't a louse; he was a world-class louse!

Which reminded her, she'd have to call her father.

Of all the calls Mary Beth Williams would have to make in the next few days, that was the one she dreaded most. Her father had only agreed to show up at the wedding, to give away his "darling daughter," with the utmost reluctance. And he had insisted, adamantly, that he be allowed to bring his wife. Wife Number Four. Or was it five now? Mary Beth had lost track somewhere along the way.

Her father's second marriage had lasted only a year. He was currently married to an innocuous, dishwater blonde named Sherry. Mary Beth kept mixing her up with Wife Number Three, who had been another out-of-the-bottle blonde named Sharon. No matter how hard she tried—and Mary Beth was the first to admit that she didn't try all that hard—she could never keep the two women separate in her mind. Thank goodness, she'd been in college before her father started to parade his youthful wives home for her perfunctory approval. There was no way she could ever regard any of his "women" as a stepmother, let alone as a substitute for her mother. And he knew it.

Carolyn Williams had been an extraordinary woman—in death, at the age of forty, as she had been in life. An intelligent woman. A strong woman. Her single weakness appeared to have been Gerald Williams with his smooth good looks and his even smoother and charming ways. Mary Beth had to admit that her father could be utterly charming.

She never could blame her mother for falling in love with a man who was so obviously ill-suited her. Even an intelligent woman like Carolyn Trevor Williams was entitled to one mistake. Although she was certain that her mother had never regarded her marriage to Gerald Williams as a mistake. She had been his greatest strength, just as he had truly been her greatest weakness. That was the problem, of course, when a woman of intellect married a man with little more than broad-shouldered good looks, a man with more form than substance.

Yes, her father had been a handsome devil all right. He still was now at the age of fifty-two. With that thick, luxurious mane of silver hair and those blue-green eyes, the color to make a woman weep, he attracted women without so much as lifting a finger. He was spoiled, as only a strikingly handsome man can be spoiled. He'd traded on his good looks all of his life, and they had served him well. At least in his opinion. It was beside the point if Mary Beth thought otherwise.

Never trust a handsome man any further than you can throw him. That wasn't a bad rule of thumb to live by when it came to the male of the species, Mary Beth decided as she returned to the task at hand.

She would telephone Gerald first and get the worst out of the way. That was how her grandparents had taught her to meet life's challenges. Face them, overcome them, and in the end they made you all the stronger.

Still, she dreaded making this first call, Mary Beth confessed to herself as she plunked the kitchen extension down on the table beside her and dialed the area code for Chicago.

"My dear, dear child," said Mrs. Pinchot, placing her eighty-year-old, diamond-ring-encrusted hand on Mary Beth's arm and patting it once or twice, "you've been such a brave soul through this whole ordeal. I don't understand what's gotten into young men these days. I declare I don't understand," the old woman commiserated in her Sarah Bernhardt voice before finally, and regally moving on past the table.

She didn't understand what had gotten into young men today either, Mary Beth thought, keeping a benign smile pasted on her face long after the dowager was gone. Then she turned back to her companion. "Tell me again why eating lunch at the country club is such a brilliant idea," she said through her teeth.

"Because," began the composed brunette sitting across the table from her, "because you are brave and strong and proud and undefeated. Because this is the busiest place in town for lunch and everyone who's anyone is here. Because this gives you the perfect opportunity to show them all that Mary Beth Williams can hold her head high no matter what has happened, no matter what that lousy fink has done. You're not going to give them the satisfaction of thinking you're the least bit devastated or heartbroken by this unfortunate turn of events. You may be crying on the inside, but you're going to show Greensport that you're smiling on the outside."

"Ah, yes, now I remember," Mary Beth agreed dryly. There was an edge to her voice that hadn't been there a few, short weeks ago. "As the wronged party, so to speak, I'm supposed to be a paragon of virtue and I must act like one."

Julie Metzger nodded. "Right."

Mary Beth looked affectionately at the young woman who had been her best friend since the sixth grade. She dropped her eyes and idly ran the tip of her finger around the rim of her water glass. "The truth is, Julie, I'm not heartbroken. And I do wish you'd stop referring to Jeffrey as a lousy fink." She smiled in spite of herself. "Although I admit it's an improvement on what you've been calling him for the past three weeks."

Julie lowered her voice. "If the shoe fits, I always say. The man was, and is, a bastard."

"Hello, Julie...Mary Beth..." A tall, willowy blonde they had both gone to high school with stopped by the table. "I was so sorry to hear about you and Jeffrey," she purred cattily, her eyes almost phosphorescent as they scrutinized Mary Beth, no doubt for signs of mental and physical anguish. Sheila Talbot was that sort of female. Predatory. Even when it came to her own sex. "I suppose you've heard that Jeffrey is living in Madison now with his paramour, shall we say?"

"I suppose you must say," replied Mary Beth, her brown eyes growing darker and narrowing slightly.

"I saw Jeffrey just a couple of days ago. He's apparently driving to his office here in Greensport from Madison every day." Sheila lowered her voice to a stage whisper. "And I've heard that Miss Weintraub has given him her notice."

"Bully for Miss Weintraub," Julie muttered under her breath.

Sheila Talbot made an affected little movement with her hands and sighed, "I do admire you so, Mary Beth. How very, very brave you're being."

"Oh, it's not all that difficult, Sheila," she drawled as she raised her water glass to her lips. How someone like Sheila Talbot could ever recognize bravery was beyond her. The woman didn't even have enough guts to say what was really on her mind.

The blonde's face was a study in noncomprehension at the moment. "Well, I just wanted to say that I was sorry to hear about you and Jeffrey. Everyone thought you two made such a cute couple." Fascinated, they both watched as Sheila floated on by them in a cloud of heavily scented perfume.

Cute?

Mary Beth Williams could feel the heat rising in her face. Cute! "If one more person says they're sorry about Jeffrey, if one more person tells me how brave I'm being, so help me God, I won't be responsible for my actions!"

Julie Metzger sat back in her chair and admitted, with what sounded suspiciously like a chuckle: "Trust me, in the case of Sheila Talbot, there isn't a jury in the country that would convict you."

"Oh, you're a big help," Mary Beth laughed raggedly. Then immediately sobered. "Listen, Julie, I've been doing a lot of thinking."

The brunette gave her a long, measuring look and shook her head. "You always did."

Mary Beth chose to ignore the comment. "As I said, I've been thinking and I've decided since I have two weeks of vacation coming"—neither of them wanted to be the first one to mention the word honeymoon— "I believe I'll go away for a while."

"Do you think that's wise?" Julie inquired with what she hoped was a casual air.

"I think it's very wise," Mary Beth replied, not entirely truthful. "I don't believe in running away from the situation, but I'll be damned if I'm going to sit around this town for the next two weeks when everybody knows this Saturday was supposed to be my wedding day. And then there's the lovely Caribbean honeymoon." There, she'd finally said it! It was out in the open now. "I'd like to go away for a while, Julie. I need to get away," she confessed with uncharacteristic candor.

"Do you know where you're going?"

Mary Beth nodded and leaned forward in her chair. "I don't want you to tell a soul. Promise?"

Julie quickly agreed, raising her hand in a cross-my-heart-and-hope-to-die kind of promise. "Yes, I promise."

Mary Beth allowed her enthusiasm for the idea to surface for the first time. "I thought about driving down to Chicago in the beginning." That idea was dismissed with a wave of her hand. "Then I decided I wanted to really get away from it all, and that Chicago wasn't nearly far enough away." There was something in her brown eyes that was entirely new to Julie Metzger. And here she'd thought she knew all there was to know about Mary Beth Williams. "I've always been such a reliable, sensible, practical woman, haven't I, Julie?'' her friend asked pensively, backtracking a little along the way.

What could Julie do, but agree? "You're the most reliable, sensible and practical human being I know.''

Questioning brown eyes met and held hers. "And I have survived these past three weeks with a certain amount of dignity.''

"With a great deal of dignity. And graciousness and charm and—''

"And I've refrained from speaking ill of Jeffrey,'' she interrupted the flow of compliments.

Julie Metzger raised her dark brown eyes heavenward and folded her hands in front of her. "You've been an absolute saint on the subject.''

Mary Beth went on without even pausing for a breath. "Because speaking ill of the man would have been a little like speaking ill of the dead, now wouldn't it?''

"Jeffrey should be so lucky,'' her companion mumbled under her breath.

"The town seems to be on my side,'' Mary Beth hypothesized. "For whatever that's worth.''

Julie cut straight through to the heart of the matter. "That and a quarter will get you a cup of coffee.''

Mary Beth's mouth folded in a soft, obstinate line. "Yes, and I've had about all that I can take, Julie. What does that commercial say about grabbing life with both hands and going for the gusto? Well, perhaps it's time I started going for some gusto of my own.''

Two dark eyebrows creased into a frown. "What in the world are you up to?"

Mary Beth took a deep breath and prepared to drop her little bomb. "I've decided to take the rest of the money that was put aside for the wedding and go to Las Vegas for a couple of weeks."

"Las Vegas?" Julie was stunned for a moment. "For God's sake, why?"

"Because it's the least practical, least sensible place I could think of," she said, her voice matter-of-fact. "It's bright lights and excitement and glamorous people and everything that Greensport, Wisconsin, isn't. I need something totally different and Las Vegas, Nevada, is it."

"Well, you're right about that. It certainly is different from Greensport," Julie murmured thoughtfully. Then her face began to brighten. "You know, Mary Beth, I think you may have something there. Perhaps Las Vegas is just the place for you right now. Think of the marquees flashing the names of stars and shows. A dozen different games of chance beckoning to you to try your luck. Shopping and sightseeing, fabulous restaurants and handsome men . . ."

Mary Beth appeared visibly relieved. "Then you don't think I'm crazy, do you?"

Julie shook her head and grinned. "No, you're not crazy." Then she shrugged her shoulders eloquently. "What do you have to lose? You know what they say: nothing ventured—"

Mary Beth interrupted her. "Yes, yes, I know."

Then she started to laugh with a lightheartedness she hadn't felt in years. Julie was right, of course. What did she have to lose? It was high time she learned to live a little, to enjoy the fantasy life had to offer. And what better place to enjoy the fantasy than in the glittery, rhinestone setting of Las Vegas? Who was to say—maybe she'd be unlucky in love, but lucky at cards.

Mary Beth Williams laughed again with a laugh that was warm and rich, like silk. She looked across the luncheon table with its fine Irish linen tablecloth and fine Irish linen napkins and smiled at her best friend. "You know, Julie, I'm suddenly feeling very lucky. Very lucky, indeed."

Two

———

The first time Nick Durand saw her, she was stepping into the elevator in the lobby of the Golden Nugget Hotel and Casino as he was getting out. He turned around and caught another glimpse of her as the elevator doors closed.

He wasn't sure afterward—as he stood juggling a stack of chips in his hand, elbows on the edge of the crap table—why he'd turned around for a second look.

He closed his eyes for a moment and recreated the scene in his mind. She wasn't the usual sort of woman to inspire a second look. At least not here in Las Vegas, Nevada, where glitter and glamour ruled supreme. Perhaps that was precisely why he had looked a second time.

She wasn't particularly tall or particularly glamorous or even particularly beautiful, but the lady had class. That was it. That was the word he was searching for. She was a lady and she had class. He was willing to bet on it!

Everything about her was understated, in a town where big and brassy and overstated were a way of life. Yes, she was definitely understated, from the little navy-blue dress she wore with its prim white collar and dotted swiss bow tie to her hair which was pulled into some kind of knot at the back of her head. She stood out. She was different, even here where there were Bermuda shorts from Duluth, polyester from Des Moines, rhinestone from L.A. and hustlers from just about everywhere. She was linen and she was lace and she was silk. She was the "genuine article," as his mother was fond of saying.

The second time Nick Durand saw her she was standing with one arm looped self-consciously around the bronze shoulders of the antique metal man slot machine in the Golden Nugget Casino while some obliging fellow tourist snapped her photograph. A big, burly guard was heading straight toward her. She was smiling. The guard wasn't.

Nick watched for a moment, his dark eyes both amused and bemused. There was something different about her. He was almost sure of it. Something had changed. It was her hair. She'd done something to her hair. He could swear it was shorter. And it was curling around her face in sun-streaked wisps of golden brown. The style made her look younger. Younger and softer. Too young and far too soft to be on her own in a town like Vegas.

Although it wasn't his habit to pick up unknown women, Nick almost went up to her then and introduced himself. "Excuse me," he would begin. "My name is Nicholas Durand and I'm a lawyer. Perhaps I can be of some assistance." And then, once he'd skillfully extricated her from the ironclad clutches of the law, he'd go on. "You know, I've been admiring you from across the crowded casino." He'd slip her arm through his as they strolled toward the bar at one end of the room. "And I've been wanting to introduce myself." He'd inquire what she wanted to drink before enfolding her hand in his, his thumb stroking the soft underside of her wrist as he brought her fingertips to his lips, his gaze never leaving her face even for an instant. "Look, lovely lady, this may sound like a come-on, but, dammit, I can't seem to take my eyes off you."

Only he didn't. He didn't say a word of it, of course. And he didn't go up to her.

It wasn't his style for one thing. And he had to confess that he was probably spoiled. Women usually came to him. He could even spot in an instant one who was trying to play hard to get because she thought that *that* was the way to get through to him. But while a dozen other women of every shape and size had given him the once-over since he had stepped off the elevator a few hours earlier—it always amazed him how aggressive some women could be—this woman simply hadn't seen him. It was no act either. She'd never once raised her eyes to look at him, surreptitiously or otherwise. Perhaps she was nearsighted, he speculated, and too vain to wear her glasses.

At that, Nicholas Durand chuckled. Talk about vain! Face it, Nick old boy, the woman just doesn't see you!

And that somehow irritated Nick Durand, age thirty-two on his last birthday, as nothing else could have. He was not a man reconciled to being ignored.

He was tall—a full six feet tall in his bare feet. He was cut lean like a man who earned his pay riding herd, and yet he was surprisingly broad in the shoulders and muscular. He was as smooth as twelve-year-old Scotch and went down just as easily. He looked equally at home in a three-piece suit or a pair of well-washed Levis and a faded chambray shirt. Cowboy boots were, of course, optional.

He was a decidedly handsome man and he knew it, but he rarely thought about it. It would be like consciously thinking about the color of your eyes. What was, in short, was. Thinking about it was a waste of time.

He had more important things on his mind right now, like the delicate flush on the young woman's cheeks as the security guard explained the "no photos" policy to her. It made sense from the management's point of view. It was easier to say "no photographs allowed" than to try to distinguish between the innocent tourist from Muskegon with his Canon Sureshot, and the not-so-innocent snoop. Or worse. In the long run, Nick supposed, it avoided a lot of hassle.

Later, he saw the lady seated at a two-dollar black-jack table, a paperback copy of *A Guide to Casino Gambling* clasped in her hand and a pile of one-dollar chips stacked neatly in front of her.

Big-time spender, Nick laughed gently as he stood there watching her decide whether to "hold" or take a "hit."

He watched her play several hands. Sometimes she won and sometimes she lost, but she seemed to be beating the odds. The stack of chips in front of her slowly grew. Beginner's luck, no doubt about it.

A quarter of an hour later, Nick was still reminding himself it was time to mosey along. And he would have, too—or so he told himself—when a slick-looking type suddenly stopped behind the lady and said something to her. Whatever it was, it flustered her. It only took a matter of seconds to see why. The man leaned over her shoulder and plunked down a sizable stack of one-hundred-dollar bills on the table in front of her own comparatively conservative bet of two dollars.

Nick felt the hair at the base of his skull stand straight on end. He put his shoulders back and brought himself up to his full height of six feet two inches, *including* boots. He didn't like it one bit. Talk about leading an innocent lamb to the slaughter! How was she supposed to defend herself in a town like Vegas with its high rollers from oil-rich Kuwait and international-banking Hong Kong? What was she doing here all by herself anyway? She may have fussed with her hair and put a little makeup on, but that didn't assure instant sophistication. Someone ought to keep an eye on the girl for her own protection, and he didn't mean the handsome sheikh-type who was moving in on his territory now. Damn, he wanted to thrash the man! If the guy so much as laid a finger on her, Nick knew he would be tempted to beat him to a pulp.

Nick Durand's mouth curved in disbelief as he stared down at his hands. They were clenched into two hard fists at his sides. What the hell was wrong with him? He didn't know the woman, and he certainly didn't owe her anything. In fact, he'd be crazy to get mixed up with her. But he knew he wasn't just going to walk away and leave her to the mercy of God knows what. He just couldn't do it.

Nick laughed at himself, but it wasn't particularly funny. If the people back in Elko County could see him now, they'd certainly have their doubts about the highly respected Nicholas James Durand, attorney-at-law. It wasn't like him to lose his cool, especially when it came to a woman.

Yes, back in Elko he had a certain reputation with the ladies; some of it deserved, some of it not. Either way, it was no skin off Nick's nose. He was damned good at what he did and that's all that mattered to him.

Beneath the sleek, smooth, and sometimes deceptively fast-talking lawyer, people back home knew he was tough, they knew he was a man. A man like his dad and his granddad. A man who would go down to the line to help a friend.

There were plenty of times when Nick felt like an old-time circuit preacher, or a frontier judge, riding from place to place, from client to client, giving aid, hearing confessions, giving succor to lost souls. Sometimes he was compensated in hard, cold cash. Just as often it came in the form of fresh eggs or a side of beef.

He wasn't rich, at least he didn't think so, but he did well enough for himself. He drove a Ford Ranger around the family ranch and a discreet, slate-gray, five-year-old BMW around the county on business. There were eighty thousand miles on the odometer, but what the hell, the car was probably built to go twice that far.

The Durands' territory was the northeast corner of the state, including the town of Elko, the center of Nevada's sheep- and cattle-ranching country. Walking into Nick's office was like entering a time warp; for a moment it was the year 1910 again. Clients sitting in the antique-filled room half expected to see Clarence Darrow himself walk through the door.

And little wonder. Nicholas Durand was the third generation of small-town Nevada lawyers in his family. The office had originally been his grandfather's, and then his father's. Both men were semi-retired now, and Nick shared the suite of offices with his younger brother, Matt.

The Durands had a reputation for being men with cool heads and a long fuse, a tough bunch who had survived the early days of Nevada's statehood. Nick's great-great-grandfather first came to Nevada while he was working as an engineer for the Central Pacific Railroad. The company started to build eastward through the Humboldt Valley in 1868. When the railroad was completed, the first James Durand stayed on. Eventually he married a local girl and settled down to cattle ranching.

At least one of James Durand's sons, and several of his grandsons carried on the tradition of going to an Eastern university for an education before returning to Nevada to practice law and manage the family ranch, usually with the help of a strong-minded, competent woman. Bringing a wife home from back East eventually became as much of a tradition as the law degree. Not that the Durand men chose hothouse flowers. The women were schoolteachers or the preacher's daughter. They could all sit astride a horse or cook enough food to feed an army. Sometimes they had to do both.

New blood, that's what Nick's grandfather fondly called his mother and his own beloved wife. They were both from Connecticut. He claimed they were the secret of the family's success. Whatever it was, the Durand family prospered. And they gained a reputation for being tough but fair. The Durands and their reputation went back a long, long way in the northeastern territory.

Nick's reputation back home wasn't the problem at the moment, however. His problem was one sweet, innocent young lady being confronted by a fast-talking Las Vegas hustler. She had just won four hands in a row for a grand total of eight dollars. Nick estimated that her "partner," meanwhile, had raked in several thousand dollars.

He watched, night-black eyes narrowed, as the man tried to slip her a tip of a hundred-dollar bill. He could see that at first she simply didn't understand. Then, as

the light dawned, her face became suffused with color.
Nick wasn't sure if she was angry, or embarrassed, or
both. She finally turned and spoke to the man. Whatever she said took him by surprise. Nick could see that.
The man quickly drew his hand back, along with the
crisp, green bill he'd offered her. And while he didn't
actually blush, the man did turn tail and run.

"Good girl!" Nick cheered under his breath.

It looked as if she could hold her own even here in
Sin City. Maybe she didn't need him riding shotgun
for her after all. Somehow that made him feel a little
better. And then, after a moment's thought, he realized it didn't make him feel better at all. If anything,
it made him feel worse. Had he honestly expected her
to need him to come to the rescue?

The absolute arrogance of the man! What did he
take her for anyway? Mary Beth could feel the heat
rise in her face, and she knew that she was blushing
furiously. She took a deep, sustaining breath and tried
to calm herself.

At first, she had merely been disconcerted when the
handsome stranger stepped up behind her and inquired if he could bet on her cards. What was the
proper protocol in such a case? she wondered. She'd
mumbled something, something that he obviously
took to be her consent. She certainly didn't begrudge
the man whatever he'd won. After all, it was his
money. But then to try to tip her with a hundred-dollar
bill! She had been mortified. Absolutely mortified.
Where she came from there was a name for women

who took money from men. And it wasn't very flattering.

Mary Beth Williams looked up and blushed all over again when she realized the blackjack dealer was waiting patiently for her to place her bet. She slid a small stack of chips into the designated area on the table in front of her, and waited while several other players at the table made their bets.

Then and there she vowed she wasn't going to let the incident with the stranger ruin her first evening in Las Vegas. Taking one deep breath after another, she cleared her mind of unnecessary things, feeling the characteristic calm descend upon her. Those yoga lessons at the Greensport YMCA had paid off time and again, she thought gratefully.

Now that she was relaxed, Mary Beth became aware of another sensation, some niggling sixth sense just beneath the surface. She wasn't certain how long she'd known it, but she suddenly knew she was being watched. She craned her neck and gazed up at the ceiling. She'd read somewhere that there were remote cameras and officials always watching the casinos below. She also knew that that wasn't it. It wasn't that kind of disinterested observation. No, someone was *really* watching her.

While the dealer went through the process of shuffling the cards and replacing them in the rectangular box called a shoe—no small feat since most Las Vegas casinos now used six decks of cards—she casually turned halfway around in her seat and made a pretense of studying the numbers flashing up on the Keno board behind her.

There was a charge of kinetic energy, of excitement, in the Golden Nugget Gambling Hall tonight. The sparkle of the crystal chandeliers overhead, the richness of the wine-colored carpeting underfoot, the sounds of clinking coins and busy slot machines, the shouts of encouragement from those gathered around a crap table with a hot roller, the spin of the roulette wheel, all added to the feeling of exhilaration.

As Mary Beth's gaze swept across the dazzling Gay Nineties casino, exciting and noisy and milling with people as it was, she pulled herself up short. There, not more than twenty feet away from her, she encountered a pair of dark, dark watchful eyes.

And, oh, what eyes! They were as black and as fathomless as a desert night without stars. They were fringed by long, sooty eyelashes and set in a deeply tanned face. And they were watching her. Closely. Intently.

No, not another one! she groaned as her mind unconsciously registered the vital statistics. The man was tall and lean, dark-haired and handsome. Yes, he was decidedly handsome. He was wearing a three-piece suit in some expensive-looking material; a wafer-thin gold watch on his wrist and a pair of hand-tooled, leather... cowboy boots? Good God, this one was a cowboy! There was a cowboy on her trail. Mary Beth almost laughed out loud.

What was it with the men in Las Vegas anyway? Yes, she'd had her hair cut and styled. And, yes, she had followed the beauty consultant's advice with her makeup. The new silk dress she'd bought that afternoon fit her to perfection, and the vivid shade of rose was flattering to her. But she was still the same woman, Mary Beth decided. Essentially she hadn't changed. She had never been the kind of female to garner male attention as if it were somehow her due. She wasn't the first woman a man noticed when he came into a room, but she liked to think that she was the one who lingered in his mind afterward.

She just might have to alter the image she'd always had of herself, she thought with a wry smile. First an amorous sheikh, now a handsome cowboy fresh off the range. Not that she'd ever seen a cowboy dressed like this one, and his "range" was probably some board room overlooking downtown Dallas or greater Los Angeles. Perhaps she wasn't the only one trying to live a little fantasy in this desert oasis of bright lights and even brighter nights.

Mary Beth forced her eyes to leave the man and return to the pair of cards face down on the table in front of her. She picked up the first card the dealer had given her. It was the ace of diamonds. Then she glanced at the second: the seven of spades. She now had a total of eight or eighteen, since an ace was always counted as one or eleven in the game of blackjack or twenty-one. She was suddenly unsure of what she should do. Was it best to take another card or not?

Mary Beth was certain she hadn't spoken out loud, and yet the answer came from directly behind her in a deep, masculine voice. A voice that somehow reached out and touched her; a voice that resounded through her flesh right down to her bones; one that she was sure could convince the greatest skeptic of the truth, the most recalcitrant to cooperate, and the coldest woman of its warmth.

"Statistically, the odds are slightly in your favor if you don't take another card on a soft eighteen when the dealer has a deuce showing," drawled the masculine voice. "Of course you have to play your own hunches."

"Thank you," Mary Beth murmured, slipping both cards under her chips to indicate to the dealer that she would play with what she had.

She was flustered, truly flustered, when the man slipped into the empty seat beside her. But it came as no surprise to her to see that it was the cowboy. She watched out of the corner of her eye as he took a slim leather wallet from his breast pocket and withdrew a handful of twenty-dollar bills.

"Five-dollar chips, please," he said to the dealer, once the hand in progress was completed and Mary Beth had been paid off for her winning cards.

The dealer smoothed the bills out in front of him on the green felt-covered table. Then he quickly counted out two identical stacks of five-dollar chips and neatly presented them to the man before depositing the cash in the drop box at his elbow. The bets were made around the table and the next hand commenced.

Mary Beth stared down at the cards placed adroitly in front of her by a well-practiced flick of the dealer's wrist. She picked up her cards and studied them. For a novice gambler like herself there was always a moment of apprehension as she added up the total. This time she was holding a queen and an ace. That added up to twenty-one. Good Lord, wasn't that blackjack?

Mary Beth tried quickly to remember what she'd read: a blackjack was any original two-card hand containing an ace and a ten-value card, like a king, queen, jack, or ten. A card like the queen of hearts she was holding in her hand. Yes, she had blackjack! All of a sudden, her mind went blank. Now what was she supposed to do? Damn, what *else* had the book said?

"I—I can't seem to remember what to do if I have blackjack," she ventured in a tentative voice, turning to the man beside her. "Am I supposed to turn my cards over right away?"

The cowboy smiled at her, his teeth ivory-white against the healthy-looking tan he sported. "Yup, and you get paid one and a half times your bet, little lady." He glanced down at the two one-dollar chips in front of her. "In your case, that means you win three dollars." There was an audible groan from someone at the other end of the table. "Now my initial bet happens to be ten dollars. If I had blackjack, I could win an additional fifteen." The cowboy glanced down at his cards and neatly slid them under his bet without disturbing the chips. "But I don't happen to have your luck."

"Do you work here?" Mary Beth inquired several minutes later as the dealer's attention turned to the other players.

"No, ma'am." He tipped an imaginary cowboy hat back from his forehead. "And I'm not a shill either."

"A shill?"

Eyes like the nighthawk looked at her long and hard. "A shill is someone who works for the casino and poses as a player in order to speed up the action when things get a little slow. It's perfectly legal," he assured her.

"Oh, I see." Mary Beth suddenly felt a little like Alice in Wonderland. Things were not always what they seemed to be, especially here in Las Vegas. She would do well to remember that.

"What about you? Are you here on vacation?" the man asked as he raised his hand and signaled for a cocktail waitress.

"Yes, I am." She gave him a meaningful look as the pretty waitress in the thigh-high skirt promptly came in response to his call.

"The lady will have a—"

Mary Beth said the first thing that popped into her mind. "A daiquiri, please."

"And I'll have a Chivas and water." His tanned face dissolved into a heart-stopping smile that brought a faint blush to the young waitress's cheeks. No doubt their drinks would arrive momentarily, Mary Beth thought wryly. "We haven't had the pleasure of introducing ourselves," the man continued cordially. "My name is Nicholas Durand. My friends call me Nick."

She just bet they did. "I'm Mary Beth Williams," she said after a slight hesitation.

"You mentioned that you were here on vacation, Miss Williams," he said, lifting one dark eyebrow. "Where are you from?"

"Greensport, Wisconsin," she replied equably. "It's a small town about thirty miles from Madison. And you?"

"I'm from up around Elko County, that's in northeastern Nevada. Elko's a small town thirty miles from nowhere," he said, his voice as warm and as dry as the June night air in the desert city.

Mary Beth turned as the cocktail waitress served her drink on a small paper napkin, and then that of the man beside her. She couldn't help but notice the generous tip that Nick Durand slipped into the girl's hand. Drinks were on the house as long as a patron was gambling, but it was considered a matter of courtesy to tip the waitress for her services. Mary Beth had read all about it in one of the colorful pamphlets the travel agent had sent her before she left home.

"Thank you for the drink," she murmured, taking a sip of her icy daiquiri. She hadn't realized how thirsty she was.

"You're welcome, Miss Williams," came the man's voice, light with nonchalance. "As a matter of fact, I've been wanting to have a drink with you all evening." His admission took her by surprise, and he knew it. "I've been watching you play blackjack."

"Yes, I know." She suddenly realized it was true. "You're a pretty smooth operator for a cowboy, aren't you, Mr. Durand?" she laughed as she took another sip of her drink.

He stared down into the glass of amber-colored Scotch, and then raised his eyes to hers. "Yes, ma'am."

Her eyebrows went up even further in surprise. Then she somehow found the audacity to say, "And I'll wager that you've never been anywhere near a ranch."

"I'm afraid you'd lose that bet, Miss Williams. There is a family ranch; it's called the Triple D. But the truth is, I'm only a part-time cowboy."

"Ah . . ." It was a very telling "ah." "And what do you do, Mr. Durand, besides punch cows, or whatever it is that cowboys do in this day and age?"

He looked her straight in the eye. A muscle in his face started to twitch ever so slightly in an effort not to smile. "I'm a lawyer."

Mary Beth noticed that he'd lost most of his down-home accent somewhere along the way. "Ah, yes, a lawyer."

This was a far less telling "ah," at least in Nick's estimation. "Law is generally considered a honorable profession, Miss Williams."

"There are no honorable professions, Mr. Durand, only honorable or dishonorable men," she said, a shade haughtily.

The man's eyes widened appreciably as he muttered, "Good Lord, you must be a schoolteacher."

Mary Beth nearly choked on her drink. "Worse than that, I'm afraid. I'm a librarian."

Before he could reply, the dealer interrupted their conversation. "Would you care to place a bet for this hand, miss?" he inquired politely, bringing their attention back to the game.

"Yes, of course," Mary Beth murmured, pushing a stack of chips toward the center of the table. She was too flustered to bother counting. It wasn't until she'd had a chance to collect her wits that she realized she had just bet ten dollars on a single deal of the cards. Oh well, easy come, easy go, she thought as she waited for the hand to conclude. She should have known better than to be distracted by the man in the first place. Wasn't she the one who'd said it wasn't wise to trust a handsome man any farther than a girl could throw him? Well, she figured she couldn't budge this man more than an inch at best. And that's exactly how far she'd trust him—one inch.

But she did win the hand, and the next and the next.

"It looks like we're good luck for each other," Nick murmured as they were paid off for their third winning hand in a row. They'd both made a tidy profit for themselves in the space of a few minutes.

"In that case, why tempt fate?" Mary Beth said, gathering up her chips and scooping them into her handbag.

"Cash me in, please," Nick said to the dealer, trading his five- and ten-dollar chips in for a smaller stack of higher denomination.

"Color change," the dealer called out to the pit boss behind him as he made the exchange.

Mary Beth gave a little sigh and stretched her legs as she stepped away from the blackjack table into the crowd perpetually milling around a major downtown casino on a Friday night. Not that you could always tell day from night in Las Vegas. That was part of the fantasy as well—no windows in the casinos—just bright lights and time standing still.

She felt a firm hand grasp her by the elbow and glanced up to see Nick Durand beside her. She gave another little sigh. God knows the man was handsome—and smooth. Far too polished to be a cowboy.

She could see that now. She wondered if there were gangsters this far west.

Probably not. But it was rather fun to think of him as a cowboy one minute and a gangster the next. She could imagine whatever she wanted to; it was her fantasy. And Nicholas Durand had himself no doubt imagined the staid lady librarian taking her glasses off, letting her long hair down and turning into some kind of ravishing creature. Perhaps it hadn't happened exactly that way with either of them, but they were both allowed to fantasize a little, surely.

All of a sudden, Mary Beth realized she was walking simply to be walking, with no destination in mind. And Nick Durand was walking right along with her. It was time for them to part company. She might find him interesting, perhaps even a bit fascinating, but she couldn't afford to get mixed up with a man like this one. She'd had her fill of smooth, charming, handsome men a long, long time ago.

"I did appreciate the advice back at the blackjack table, Mr. Durand. I'm afraid I don't know much about gambling." Mary Beth stopped and extended her hand. "Thank you for your help."

The man took her hand and held it lightly in his without shaking it. He smiled down into her face, his own open and unbeguiling. "Why don't we have another drink together and try our luck at Keno?" he suggested, indicating the lounge behind them. It was a delightful room decorated in comfortable, Florida-style wicker furniture. "I think we'd make an unbeatable team." Then he smiled at her again and she was lost.

Lord, he could tempt the angels themselves, Mary Beth rationalized as she felt her head bob up and down in agreement. She allowed herself to be escorted into the Keno lounge before voicing her ignorance of the game. "Is Keno very complicated?"

"Heck, no. In fact, it's a lot like bingo." Nick settled her on a cushioned sofa and sat down beside her. He picked up a pad of forms from the coffee table in front of them before he continued. "Each Keno ticket has the numbers one to eighty printed on it." Mary Beth could see that immediately. "You decide how many numbers you want to play and how much you want to bet, and then you mark them on a ticket with a black crayon."

"Is that all there is to it?"

"Not quite," he answered, his voice moving on, quietly, slowly, like fingers tiptoeing up her spine. "Next, we take our marked ticket up to the counter and the man punches out an official form with our numbers. When the game is closed, the bingo blower behind the counter is turned on and twenty of the eighty Ping-Pong balls inside pop out, one by one. As each number is announced, it flashes up on the tally boards all over the casino."

"I wondered what the numbers were in the restaurant at lunch today," Mary Beth stammered, very much aware of the man beside her and the long line of his thigh against hers.

"They're everywhere," Nick concurred. "Now, let's say we pick nine numbers and bet a dollar. If five of our numbers are chosen, we'd win about five dollars." He leaned closer and showed her one of the numerous pamphlets that listed the odds and the winning money. "If all nine of our numbers come up, we could win over six thousand dollars."

Mary Beth gave the man a quick smile, and reminded herself to breathe. "The odds of that happening must be astronomical."

Nick leaned back against the sofa cushions. "The best way to think of the game of Keno is as a pleasant way to rest your feet, have a cool drink and lose your money."

"Well, my feet are comfortable and here comes the cocktail waitress, so that only leaves losing my money," Mary Beth pointed out. "How do you propose we go about choosing our nine lucky numbers?"

With dark brows furrowed, Nick appeared to be considering her question. "Well, I've always said that the best Keno numbers are the ones that mean something to those gambling. I think we should pick numbers that have some personal meaning. So why don't we start with our ages? Ladies first, of course."

Mary Beth saw the momentary wicked look that flitted across his handsome features. The man seemed inordinately pleased with himself. Not that she minded telling him her age. She didn't mind in the least. For one thing, she was willing to bet that he was several years older than she was. "I'm twenty-seven."

"Twenty-seven," Nick repeated as he picked up a black crayon from a tray on the coffee table and made an *X* through the number twenty-seven. "And I'm thirty-two," he added as he made a second mark. "Lots of people use dates like wedding anniversaries, but neither of us is married." He paused for a fraction of a second as if he were giving her the perfect opportunity to contradict him—should she be so inclined.

"No, neither of us is married," Mary Beth echoed. "I don't suppose either of us ever has been."

Nick shook his head; it wasn't necessary for him to say a word. But she almost blurted out then and there that it had been a pretty close call for her. She was one day away from what would have been her wedding day. But those memories were difficult to keep in her head here in Las Vegas as she sat beside a strikingly handsome man, having a drink. If she looked close enough, Mary Beth could make out the character lines on his forehead, at the corners of his eyes and mouth, that saved him from being just a little too pretty, just a little too handsome. She was grateful for those lines, each and every one of them.

"I suppose we could use the month and the day we were born," Nick was suggesting when she failed to come up with any brilliant suggestions of her own. "In my case that would be three and fifteen."

"Your birthday is March fifteenth?" she translated, her brow wrinkling. "'Beware the ides of March,'" she murmured under her breath. Was it meant as some kind of warning?

"When is your birthday?" she heard the man inquire, his crayon posed above the Keno ticket.

"October...October thirteenth. That's—"

"Ten and thirteen," Nick announced before she had a chance to finish. "Let me see, that's six numbers. We need three more. How many brothers and sisters do you have?'' He glanced up at her, hopeful.

She did hate to rain on his parade. "None. How about you?"

"One brother and one sister for a grand total of two."

"That's our next number then." Mary Beth watched as he made another X on the Keno ticket. "Wait a minute, I don't have any siblings, but my father has had four wives," she piped up as she took a long drink of the daiquiri the waitress had served her only moments earlier.

Nick gave her an odd little look and proceeded to mark off the number four. "And I think we should use sixteen as our last lucky number," he said, not altogether seriously.

"Why sixteen?" Mary Beth inquired.

Two dark desert eyes found and held hers for a moment. "Because you and I met today, and today is the sixteenth of June."

How romantic...Mary Beth shook her head and wondered if she'd inadvertently spoken out loud. She couldn't tell from the expression on Nick Durand's face. He was busy fishing around in his wallet for a dollar bill.

"Wait a minute," she called out unnecessarily. She quickly opened her handbag, dug around in the bottom and came up with a one-dollar chip. "Please allow me this time, Nick. You've been overly generous tipping the waitress each time she brings us our drinks." Her face was a little bit pink as she dropped the chip into his palm. Pink and warm. Although whether it was from the two daiquiris she'd had or simply self-consciousness on her part, even Mary Beth wasn't certain. "Please..."

"All right, thanks," Nick accepted the chip from her and got to his feet. He seemed to understand that she wanted to maintain her independence by paying her share. "I'll go place our bet, and then I'll be right back."

She watched him walk toward the counter and take a place in one of the lines. He was a head taller than anyone else. But it wasn't only his six feet plus of height that made Nick Durand stand out. Admittedly, it was the first thing one noticed, but the eye lingered because of the way his well-tailored clothes hugged his beautifully formed body. The eye lingered over the expanse of broad shoulder because it promised to taper to nothing less than a lean, hard waist. His hands were large and well-formed, his arms muscular and, no doubt, as tanned as his face.

Nicholas Durand was the best-looking man she'd ever met. The question was, what was he doing here. And that's precisely what Mary Beth asked him as soon as he returned and settled back down on the sofa beside her.

"So what's a lawyer from Echo County doing here in Las Vegas?"

"It's Elko County, E-L-K-O," he corrected her. "I flew down on business for the law firm and, like you, decided to stay a few extra days on vacation. My brother, Matt, is minding the store. That's one advantage of a family business," he told her affably, crossing one muscular leg over the other, and flicking at an imaginary speck of dust on his well-polished cowboy boots. "What kind of librarian are you?"

"If I were working in a university or city library, I suppose I would be described as a research librarian," she said, straightening. "In a town the size of Greensport, a librarian does a little bit of everything from checking out books to children's story hour to answering questions."

"So you're a research librarian..."

"There isn't a joke or double entendre that I haven't heard a hundred times, Nick," she said good-humoredly, warning him off.

He appeared innocent enough as he skirted the issue. "What kinds of questions do you get?"

Mary Beth grinned. "You wouldn't believe me if I told you."

"Try me."

"Well, some of the questions are routine, like 'Who was the first man on the moon?' or 'What is the sister galaxy to our own Milky Way?'" She answered her own questions before he even attempted to do so. "That's Neil Armstrong, and the Andromeda Galaxy, of course."

"Of course," he murmured, suitably impressed. "What else do you get asked?"

She laughed lightly to herself. "One time I was asked if my face hurt."

"If your face hurt?" he repeated, frowning. "What did you say?"

"No, and then the caller said, 'That's funny, because it's killing me.'"

"Oh no, not that old joke," Nick groaned.

"Yes, that old joke." Mary Beth could barely contain herself. She started to titter, just a little at first and way back in her throat. But the more she thought about it, the funnier it all got until she dissolved into unrestrained laughter.

"You may not be good at jokes," Nick said once she'd quieted down again, "but I'll bet you're one hell of a 'Trivial Pursuit' player." He rubbed his hands together with relish, as if he were really onto something big here. "Boy, with you on my team, we could wipe Matt and his wife, Kit, off the face of the earth." And he sounded positively delighted at the prospect.

Mary Beth was fascinated. "Do I detect a note of sibling rivalry in your voice?"

"I wouldn't exactly call it sibling rivalry. It's more like a good, old-fashioned competition between brothers. You see, I've had one deuce of a time finding just the right partner for my team. I don't like to lose."

"No, I don't imagine that you do." Mary Beth looked up and noticed the bingo blower was tossing Ping-Pong balls to and fro in preparation for choosing the twenty numbers. "And speaking of winning or losing..." Several minutes later, there was no doubt in either of their minds that they'd lost. Only three of their nine numbers even made a show on the tally board. "Let's have another drink and try again," she suggested gaily, raising her hand to signal the cocktail waitress.

"I have a better idea," Nick intervened, grasping her by the hand and lowering her arm. "It's almost nine o'clock and I'll wager that you haven't had any dinner."

Mary Beth's eyes were blank with astonishment. "Food?"

"Yes, food," he said patiently. "There's a great little sushi bar just around the corner. Let's grab something to eat and then we'll come back and play our lucky numbers again later."

"Sushi as in raw fish sushi?" Mary Beth asked incredulously as Nick unfolded his long legs and stood up. He held his hand out to her.

"Actually, sushi means rice. Sashimi means raw fish. Have you ever tried it?"

"No, we don't have a lot of call for raw fish in Greensport," she said with a snicker.

"Well, I think you'll be pleasantly surprised and I'm sure you'll enjoy it," Nick assured her as they wound their way through the crowded casino. "By the way," he went on, once they were outside and strolling along arm-in-arm through the warm night air. "There's something I'd like to ask you—if you wouldn't consider it too personal."

Mary Beth looked around her, surprised—and yet not in the least surprised—to find herself on her way to dinner with the man. "I won't know if it's too personal until you ask me," she pointed out with indisputable logic.

Nick cleared his throat and looked as though he was about to present his case to the jury. "Earlier this evening, a slick oil-sheikh type came up and started betting on your cards."

"Yes, I wasn't even sure if he was allowed to do that, but the dealer didn't say anything." She stopped and stared up at him. "I'm sorry. I interrupted you. What was your question?"

Nick raked his fingers through his hair. "What in the world did you say to the man to send him scurrying off like that?"

She stared at him. "That's your question?"

"Yes."

Mary Beth was tempted not to tell him and let his imagination run wild. She was sure it would be far more interesting than the truth. But he didn't look like the type who enjoyed being teased. She relented, and decided to tell him. "I told him that my fiancé wouldn't like it if I took money from another man."

Nick was disbelieving. "That's all?"

"Not quite," she said evasively. "I also told him that my fiancé was twice his size and violently jealous of anyone who dared so much as to look at me."

"Nice touch," Nick chuckled as they started walking along the sidewalk again. He could take a joke as well as the next man. "And is he?"

"And is he *what*?"

"And is your fiancé twice the size of that oil sheikh and violently jealous of you?"

Mary Beth swallowed. "Yes and no."

Nick stopped chuckling and came to a halt. What the hell did she mean "Yes and no"? What fiancé? He'd been joking! "What the hell do you mean?" he croaked.

She hadn't meant to tell him in quite this way, but the expression on his face left Mary Beth with the distinct feeling that a quick explanation was called for. "Yes, my fiancé—or I should say my ex-fiancé—was twice the guy's size. But, no, he was too reasonable, he had too much common sense to be violently jealous of me. It wasn't Jeffrey's style."

"And just when did this...this Jeffrey become your ex-fiancé?" Nick demanded to know. Whether he had the right to demand or not never became an issue between them.

"About a month ago," Mary Beth murmured, studying the sidewalk beneath their feet.

"And little wonder if he didn't have the common sense, or the guts, to hang on to what was his," Nick declared.

How odd. The man just naturally assumed that she was the one who'd dumped Jeffrey, instead of the other way around.

"But..."

"Come on, Mary Beth," Nick drawled, the tensed muscles of his body beginning to relax as he spotted the sushi bar. "It's time you took the plunge, and I'm just the man for the job." He put an arm around her shoulders. "Trust me, you're going to love the food here."

"Don't bet on it," Mary Beth muttered under her breath as she was whisked through the door of the restaurant.

Three

—

"All right, all right, you win!"

Mary Beth made a little gesture of resignation with her hands as they emerged from the restaurant an hour, perhaps even two hours later. She wasn't sure what time it was, and she decided that she didn't care to know. She had already learned that time has very little meaning in Las Vegas.

"I win?" Nick teased as he slipped an arm around her waist, tucking her into his side as they strolled along Fremont Street.

"Yes, you win," she repeated, resting her head on his shoulder.

The sights and sounds of nighttime Las Vegas were all around them: loud music pouring out of open doorways, the familiar ring of electronic slots and metal coins clinking against metal machines, the

shouts of encouragement and the groans of dismay.
Here and there they passed a small, dingy casino,
usually located next to a pawnbroker's shop. But there
were stars in Mary Beth's eyes and she chose to see
only what she wanted to see. And that did not include
a third-rate gambling joint with a hawker out in front,
or a pathetic display of cameras in the dirt-stained
window of a pawnshop.

They stopped at the street corner by the Golden
Nugget and looked across to the Four Queens Hotel.
"I hear there's a good lounge singer performing at the
Four Queens. Why don't we stroll over and see if we
can find a table?" Nick suggested.

Her first instinct was to look down at her watch and
make some comment about the late hour, but Mary
Beth caught herself in time and resisted the urge. This
was Las Vegas, it came alive at night while other cities slept; cities like Greensport, Wisconsin. It was the
reason she'd decided to come here in the first place. To
be someplace different, to do something different, to
break out of her normal routine and live a little. Why
not now? And why not with a handsome man who
genuinely seemed to enjoy her company? Yes, Nick
Durand might be deemed dangerous by her usual
standards of judging men, but didn't that make him
all the more exciting, like Las Vegas itself?

"It sounds like a wonderful idea," she murmured,
indulging herself for a moment by pressing her face
into his suit jacket. The material was soft and fine; it
smelled deliciously like the man—a faint blend of
Scotch and citrus after-shave and something less de-
finable that somehow reminded her of the desert at

of the sparkling wine. He poured himself a glass and raised it in the air. "I'd like to propose a toast."

"A toast to what, Mr. Durand?"

"A toast to Lady Luck...may she always be as good to us as she has been tonight."

"To Lady Luck then."

They sat and sipped their champagne, talking in low voices, sometimes falling silent to listen to the soft, seductive music playing somewhere in the background. They were vaguely aware of the indistinct hum of other people conversing in the intimate bar, but they only had eyes for each other.

"This champagne is delicious," Mary Beth blurted out as Nick topped off her glass. "What vintage is it?" Then absentmindedly she went on, "You know, I've been thinking about revamping my entire wardrobe, Nick. From now on I'll wear nothing but silks and safari clothes."

The man frowned at the quantum leap in their conversation. Silks and safari clothes? Where had that come from? What had happened to their discussion of champagne? He suddenly realized that Mary Beth might be a little tipsy. He decided the only thing to do was to go along with her and see where it led. "Silks and safari clothes in Wisconsin?"

"I'm not going to stay in Wisconsin all of my life," Mary Beth informed him calmly. "Don't get me wrong. It's not that I don't love Wisconsin. I do. But I want to see the world, Nick. I want to travel. I want to see and do it all—the British Isles, Africa, Australia. I want to stand at Stonehenge and watch the sun come up. I want to see Mount Kilimanjaro and the

Serengeti, the Great Barrier Reef and the Outback. I want to do—I want to do so very much." She fingered her glass and stared into the flaming heart of the candle. "I suppose you think I'm being silly."

"Not at all. Where would any of us be without our dreams, without the things we fantasize about doing one day?" He took a drink of his champagne. "Aren't dreams and fantasies what set man apart from the other animals? Without our dreams, we're little more than animals ourselves." He paused, then probed very gently. "Do you have any dreams of marrying and having children one day? Or did what's-his-name sour you on men altogether?"

"Who, Jeffrey?" she hooted lightly. "You have to understand something, Jeffrey Donnell's a CPA: a certified pain in the..." Mary Beth quickly clamped a hand over her mouth. "Oops! That's what my best friend, Julie, always calls him."

"You haven't answered my question," Nick pointed out.

She looked at him and frowned. "I seem to have forgotten what your question was."

"Do you still plan to get married someday and have children?"

Mary Beth brightened. "Of course I do. But I have to meet the right man first." Elbows on the edge of the table, she settled her chin in her hands. "And do you have your dreams, Nick Durand?"

His face was masked by darkness. For a moment she thought he wasn't going to answer her. Then he opened his mouth and began to speak, his voice growing softer and softer, his words weaving a spell around her, almost caressing her. "Oh, yes, I have my dreams, Mary Beth." The word vibrated on the tip of his tongue. "I dream about finding the right woman to love. I dream about seeing my sons and daughters grow up on the Triple D, learning to love the land as I did when I was growing up." He paused and the intimacy of the night seemed to surround them. "Sometimes I fantasize about having enough time one day to take up photography, and maybe even have my own darkroom."

She sensed there was more. "And..."

"And sometimes I dream about sitting down and writing a book about my experiences as a small-town lawyer."

Mary Beth was certain she was the first person Nick had told and it made her glow inside. There was something very special about sharing a dream with someone. In a funny kind of way, she had shared more of herself with this man than she ever had with Jeffrey. Not that she'd shared a whole heck of a lot with Jeffrey Donnell now that she thought about it. That was the problem with being from a "good family," of course. One had to be good. It was expected. Back home, a Williams didn't, *couldn't*, do so many things. She and Jeffrey had known each other for nearly a year. They had dated for three months before becoming engaged. Their engagement had lasted a mere two months. When all was said and done, Mary Beth realized they were just as much strangers at the end as they had been in the beginning. She knew Jeffrey's shirt size and his sleeve length and even his social security number, but she knew nothing about his dreams, about the crazy schemes he plotted in his head late at night while the rest of the world was asleep.

Did he ever rise from his bed and steal away into the mist-covered garden behind his house when the moon was full? She did. Did he ever take a book of childhood poetry from the shelf and linger over the familiar verses and pictures that came back like old friends visiting on a Sunday afternoon? Did he keep a small treasure box way, way in the back of the bottom drawer of his bureau? A box filled with little trinkets won at the county fair, or a special stone rubbed smooth at the bottom of the creek in the park, or a faded postcard of some faraway place that he had visited only in his dreams?

Dear God, how mismatched she and Jeffrey had been!

She was amazed. If they had married, they would have made each other miserable. They brought out the worst in each other. They were too careful, too controlled when they were together. There hadn't been any spontaneity. There hadn't been any joy. And there had been no real passion between Jeffrey and herself. Why hadn't she seen that before? Why was she only truly understanding it all now? And why here on a warm summer's night, a thousand miles away from home, while she was with another man, a man who was getting to his feet and holding his hand out to her, asking her to dance?

Somehow that one strong hand beckoning to her was more enticing than another man's offer of riches and jewels. Mary Beth felt herself inescapably drawn to him. She floated to her feet and into Nick Durand's arms as he whispered in her ear, "I think you'll like dancing in the dark."

She drew in a long breath and let it out slowly. He had a clean, masculine aroma of leather and the sun burning into hot, desert sand. He was like the unyielding hardness of scorched earth, the tough native sagebrush, the adventure of a land still untamed.

As Mary Beth came into his arms, Nick filled his lungs with her fragrance. It was subtle, surprisingly sensuous, slightly fruity with a touch of musk. He inhaled again. She made him think of something cool and crisp and apple tart. Somehow she was like the rolling, green Wisconsin hills where she came from, reminding him of lush grass and deep-blue skies.

He could feel the faint flutter of her pulse where his thumb skimmed her wrist. He could almost make out the telltale hint of blue veins against porcelain skin on the sensitive underside. He watched as if from high above as he drew her hand to his mouth and brushed his lips along that sensitive skin. He felt her draw in her breath, he felt her pulse race, and he felt the rising heat in his own blood.

A tiny cry seemed to escape her before she could stop it. And then she said his name wistfully, fearfully, with her heart pounding against his. "Nick—"

"I know, sweetheart, I know," he was desperate enough to say.

Nick buried his face in her hair. She smelled of moonlight. His hands glided down her back and around the curve of her derriere. She was like silk in his hands. It was all there in his grasp—the soft, elegant, woman's body; the silk texture of her dress; the dream of smooth, silky skin beneath.

His imagination took off without him. She would be so sweet to love. Sweet and hot. Buried somewhere deep within her, there was a passion waiting, smoldering, ready to burn white-hot if the right man loved her in the right way. He could sense it. He could feel it. He was certain of it. She would catch fire and consume a man, and he would gladly die in the heat of that passion.

Nick could feel her flow through his hands like hot, liquid gold. He could feel her lovely body moving beneath the cool, silk dress. How could she be so hot and yet so cool? He had the crazy urge to tear the silk dress from her body and reveal the secrets underneath. He wanted to lose himself in her, to run his hands slowly over her body, to bring her into the rising heat of his thighs, to relieve the strange ache building inside him, to feel the fullness of her breasts as they pressed against his chest, their tips hard and aroused.

He felt a groan rise from his chest and settle in his throat, nearly choking him with its urgency, with a desperate need to be voiced. "My God, Mary Beth, dancing with you is torture, such sweet torture," he rasped tightly.

Nick slipped one hand around her waist, the other clasped her right hand and held it chest-high between them. A light sheen of perspiration broke out on his forehead and upper lip, then evaporated in the cool, air-conditioned room.

It was Mary Beth who broke her hand free of his and raised it to his shoulder. She slipped both of her hands around to the back of his neck, entangling them in his hair as her fingers interlaced. Nick's left hand was pressed between them. And that's when he realized his palm was just above her breast. If he were to move it a fraction of an inch...Mary Beth must know it, too. She had to know, he told himself.

She did. She raised herself on tiptoe and whispered wine-sweetened words into his mouth. Her breath was like a summer's kiss, all honey and heat. "Touch me, Nick."

He hadn't realized how much he wanted her to say that. He hadn't known how much he wanted her to want him. God knows, he wanted her. It was crazy. It was insane. He couldn't. He shouldn't. But he wanted to touch her. He even told himself that he *needed* to touch her. Jesus, he'd lived his whole life by the letter of the law. Couldn't he relax just this once? Just this once couldn't he fantasize a little?

She's on the rebound, Nick, old boy, a little voice whispered in his mind.

Like hell she was! he swore to himself. He knew when a woman wanted *him*, and this woman did. He was willing to bet a year's worth of legal fees that she'd never been like this with that jackass Jeffrey. Maybe she'd never been like this with any man. That thought alone excited him.

"Mary Beth..." Was that strained, hoarse, questioning voice his?

"I want you to touch me, Nick. It's not loneliness. It's not even the champagne. Believe me, it's only you, only you, Nick," Mary Beth chanted softly as he finally allowed his fingers to lightly graze her breast.

He felt the quiver that rippled through her slender body at his touch. He sensed the goose bumps that broke out on her flesh. There was no mistaking the effect of his caress. Her nipples were hard, aroused, right through the layers of her clothing. He could feel one teasing him through his shirt, the other rubbing lightly against the callused skin of his palm. His hand itched. He wanted to crush her between his fingers. The unrestrained violence of his own thoughts shocked him a little.

They drifted even further into the blessed obscurity of the pitch-black dance floor. They stopped moving, dropping any pretense of dancing. They were standing there with their bodies touching from shoulder to thigh, her head resting on Nick's chest, his hands on her.

It had ceased to be a matter of right or wrong the moment she went into his arms, Mary Beth acknowledged to herself through the sensual haze that enveloped her. Her legs felt oddly heavy as they stood there, their bodies swaying slightly in time to the music. The room was cool, yet she was burning up, she could feel the red-hot heat everywhere her body touched his.

This, then, was the sweet agony of wanting and yet not having, Mary Beth thought as her mind overflowed with her body's desires. Being held, being caressed by this man was the most erotic experience of her life. She'd never felt like this before, she'd never experienced this overwhelming desire to touch and to be touched. This was need on an elemental level she had not understood until this moment. She needed

Nick Durand. It wasn't logical. It wasn't sensible, but it was true. And she wanted him. She wanted him to want her. And he did.

Just when Mary Beth despaired of ever feeling his kiss, just when his caress was quickly carrying her along on a tide of sensuality that she wasn't certain she knew how to handle, Nick lowered his head and took her mouth with his. And then she was lost in his kiss.

He kissed her and the night rushed in on them. She could discern the slightest noise, the merest movement around them. Then the room receded and there was nothing but the heat of each other's flesh, the silky scrape of her dress against his thighs, the soft, seductive feel of his jacket beneath her fingertips. She was aware of every nuance of smell and taste and touch. It was the singularly most electrifying and yet frightening moment of her entire twenty-seven years. She was no longer in control of herself, let alone the situation. Her head was swimming with sensations. It would be so easy for her to lose her head over this man.

She tried to breath. "Nick, oh God, I don't know what we're doing!"

"I do," he finally managed, tearing his mouth reluctantly from hers, but he wasn't laughing and his voice sounded strained.

"Things are getting out of hand," Mary Beth whispered, feeling his breath warm and intoxicatingly sweet on her face.

"No, no, sweet Mary Beth," he drawled in denial, but Nick knew damn well that things were getting out of hand. He just wasn't sure how it had happened.

"What if someone sees us?" she went on self-consciously.

He wanted to say that he didn't care if the whole damned city of Las Vegas saw them, but he knew that's not what Mary Beth wanted, or needed, to hear.

"It's all right, sweetheart. No one can see us back here," he murmured reassuringly as he lowered his head one last time to find her mouth.

Again, Mary Beth was lost in his kiss like an early explorer lost in an uncharted sea. Her heart was on fire, her body tingled with sensations, wild and new, her mind was strangely empty, yet she felt as though every inch of her was filled with this man, with his taste and his touch and his scent.

And, dear God, she found herself only wanting more of him!

That's when she took a step back and Nick let her go. There was danger directly ahead and they both recognized it in the same instant. Even through the semidarkness of the room, Mary Beth could see the man's chest rising and falling as though he'd just finished a marathon run. If she were to reach out and touch his face at this moment, she knew his skin would be as hot to the touch as her own. They had started a fire in each other, however innocently, however inadvertently, and now it was time to stop and put it out before the flames consumed them both.

"Nick—"

He touched his fingertips to her mouth, gently sealing her lips. His night-black eyes held hers. "No regrets, Mary Beth. Let's have no regrets."

"No regrets," she echoed, remembering his touch, his kiss.

Then there was nothing left to be said between them. The moment had come and gone. They had danced. They had kissed. They had touched, and it had almost blown up in their faces. They were a volatile combination. It could happen like that between a man and a woman. Not often, but every now and then . . . if a man and a woman were lucky.

They finished off the champagne and left the bar, strolling hand in hand down the streets of Las Vegas. The city lights were dazzling and the night was magic. They lingered in the open doorway of a casino to watch a young couple play the giant slot machine just inside in the front entrance. The oversized one-armed bandit gobbled up the couple's silver dollars until they were left with empty hands. Only real silver dollars weren't used in Las Vegas anymore, of course. Each casino had its own coins stamped out of some cheap metal alloy.

The crowd that had been cheering and groaning with the couple moved on, as did Nick and Mary Beth. Nick slipped his jacket off and slung it over one shoulder. He put his other arm around Mary Beth and it seemed the most natural thing in the world for her to slip her arm around his waist.

"Hey," she murmured, gazing toward the distant horizon. "The sky is almost tinged a shade of pink over there. Nick, the sun's coming up."

He bent over and nuzzled her neck affectionately. "It does every morning, sweetheart." He was enjoying himself. "I guess you could say we spent the night together."

Mary Beth stifled a yawn. "I've never stayed out all night. I didn't even stay out this late the night of my senior prom." Then she yawned again and snuggled up against him. "I'm so terribly sleepy, Nick."

"Let's go to bed, sweetheart." He looked down into her face. "Each of us to our own beds," he clarified as they made their way through the lobby of the Golden Nugget and into the elevator.

"What room am I in?" murmured Mary Beth drowsily.

"That's supposed to be my question," Nick laughed indulgently. "Where's your room key?"

"In my handbag, small zippered compartment on the left side," she informed him, handing over the silver beaded evening bag. "I want to thank you for the lovely dinner and the even lovelier evening, Nick," Mary Beth said as they stepped off the elevator at the sixth floor and made their way down the carpeted hallway toward her room. She might be exhausted, but that was no excuse to forget her manners.

"I had a wonderful evening and a wonderful night and a wonderful morning," he drawled.

She raised her head from his shoulder as he inserted the key into the lock and pushed open the door of her hotel room. A floor lamp stood in one corner, red velvet drapes with white lace curtains hung at the windows, and there was a red velvet settee. A king-size bed was also done up in some red tufted material.

Nick flipped the light switch beside the door, and the room was flooded with light.

Mary Beth found herself at a loss for words. "Nick, I—I..."

"I'll see you later in the day after you've had a chance to sleep for a good twelve hours," Nick said, moving a step toward her and taking her face in his hands. He gently brought her mouth up to his. For a moment, the glowing embers flared into a tiny flame between them. Then he took his mouth from hers and touched a caressing fingertip to each eye, closing them one by one. "Dream about me, sweetheart."

Then, before Mary Beth could wish him sweet dreams in return, he was gone.

Four

——

Mary Beth stood there in the lobby across from the elevators, shifting the balance of her one hundred and fifteen pounds from one strappy little high-heeled sandal to the other. The slight movement was enough to cause the skirt of her elegant dress to ripple around her long silky legs.

The dress was blue-black, taffeta and ruffled. It was also very sophisticated and exorbitantly priced. And the minute she'd laid eyes on it that afternoon, Mary Beth Williams knew she was going to buy it. She'd always dreamed of splurging on something black, something chic, something ridiculously expensive.

After all, those had been the ground rules when she decided to spend the money left over from her cancelled wedding on this trip to Las Vegas. She would only use the money for utterly frivolous and impractical things. She'd spent too much of her life being deadly serious and totally practical as it was. And what had it gotten her? A broken engagement, if not a broken heart.

No, it was time she *lived* a little. And the elegant black dress with its haute couture ruffles definitely filled the bill.

It was worth every penny, too, Mary Beth decided as she caught a glimpse of herself in the gilded mirrors to one side of the elevator doors, even if she did say so herself. She smiled at her reflection, openly amused by her own narcissism. She'd changed since coming to Las Vegas, and she liked the changes she saw in herself.

She glanced down at the slender bracelet watch on her wrist and sighed. Nick was late. Fifteen minutes late to be precise. And it wasn't like him.

She watched the elevator doors as they slid open and emptied their passengers into the lobby. Nick Durand was not among them. She let out another sigh. She was half-tempted to get a roll of quarters from the cashier circulating among the customers playing the slot machines in the hotel entrance to the casino. Then she looked down at her hands, newly manicured that afternoon, and imagined them covered with the telltale black smudges that were a sure sign that someone had been playing the slots. She decided against the idea. She wanted to look elegant tonight, perhaps even a little exotic, and dirty fingernails didn't fit the image.

Nick had told her to dress in something special for the occasion. It was their anniversary. They'd met exactly one week ago. And what a week it had been! A week filled with delicious days and delicious nights.

Good Lord, to think that she'd slept right through what would have been her wedding day! And she'd felt marvelous afterward. She remembered that night, vividly. She'd been walking out of the bathroom, her wet hair wrapped in a towel, when the telephone rang.

"Time to rise and shine, sleepyhead, your twelve hours are up!" Nick had called out cheerfully. Then his voice had grown softer, and she'd closed her eyes, almost able to imagine the shape and the feel of his mouth as he pressed it closer to the mouthpiece. "Did I wake you up?"

Mary Beth had opened her eyes and looked over at the clock on the bedside table. She'd been scandalized to see it was nearly six o'clock in the evening. "No. No, you didn't wake me up," she quickly assured the man. "I've been up for hours." But she didn't know whom she thought she was kidding. Certainly not Nick.

"You've been up for how long?" he'd teased.

"Well, maybe for an hour anyway," she had confessed, cradling the telephone receiver between her chin and shoulder, and beginning to blot at the ends of her wet hair with the terry towel. "I just stepped out of the shower."

There was a momentary silence. Then, "Once you're dried off, how about having dinner with me?"

"Only if it's my treat this time," she'd insisted.

"All right, you can treat tonight. How about checking out the latest graduates of Hamburger College?"

"Hamburger College?"

Nick had laughed then in that special way that always sent a shiver of sheer delight through her. "Yes, there's a McDonald's just down the street."

"No way, José. I'll need an hour or so to get ready, and then I'm taking you downstairs to the Lillie Langtry for dinner. I'll make the reservations as soon as we hang up."

"But—"

"There are no buts about it, Nicholas James Durand. Not if you want to have dinner with me tonight. It's my turn to treat you," she said doggedly.

"You are a persistent little cuss sometimes, aren't you?" he'd muttered, but even Nick Durand knew when it was wise to let his case rest.

And they did have a delicious dinner at the Lillie Langtry Restaurant that night. Mary Beth's treat, of course.

Then Nick had taught her, or at least *tried* to teach her, the fast-paced, action-packed game of craps, or bank craps as the dice game is officially known in Nevada. Not that Mary Beth had imagined, even in her wildest dreams, that she'd be spending her wedding night crowded around a crap table, cheering on the latest "hot roller." As it turned out, she decided it was infinitely preferable to her original plans for June the seventeenth.

As she crawled into bed that Saturday night—actually it was the wee, small hours of Sunday morning—Mary Beth realized that she hadn't thought of Jeffrey Donnell once all day. The reality of what she'd left behind in Wisconsin had very little meaning for her here. She was in Las Vegas. She was *living* the fantasy. She was having the time of her life!

On Sunday, she and Nick had lazed side by side by the hotel swimming pool. On Monday they'd taken a deluxe tour to the Grand Canyon, a scenic all-day trip flying over the spectacular natural wonder, followed by a ground tour and dinner. Yet another day had been spent boating and picnicking at nearby Lake Mead and a stagecoach ride in Old Nevada. Other days Nick had taught her the rudiments of roulette and baccarat and even a little seven-card stud. He'd taken her to see traditional Las Vegas shows like the Lido de Paris at the Stardust Hotel and the magicians Siegfried and Roy. It had been a nonstop whirl of sights and sounds and colors from beginning to end.

Sometimes it was hard for her to believe she'd been in Las Vegas for a whole week. Sometimes it was even harder for her to remember a time before this week. Las Vegas was magic, pure magic, adult style, and Nick Durand was an integral part of that magic. She never wanted it to end. She refused to think about the fact that it would, inevitably, have to end.

Where was the man? Mary Beth thought impatiently, perhaps a little frantically, tapping the toe of her high-heeled sandal on the tiled floor. The elevator doors swung open again, and she searched among the debarking passengers for that familiar dark head. Nick wasn't there.

Damn! She didn't want to think about her time with him coming to an end. Yet she knew in her heart of hearts that Nick must be pulling plenty of strings back home to get the extra days he'd spent here with her. They were living on borrowed time and they both knew it. After all, how much longer could he go on vacationing as if there were no tomorrow? It would all have to come to an end soon.

But she wasn't going to think about it right now, Mary Beth told herself. She'd think about it later. She'd think about it tomorrow.

"Yes, I'm still in Las Vegas, Matt," said Nick, propping the telephone between his ear and shoulder as he freed his hands to button the front of his dress shirt.

Then his hands stopped in midair and he stood there for a moment, listening.

"Yes, I know it's taken more time than I originally said it would. I still need a few more days here to wrap things up." He laughed into the telephone receiver as he began to button his shirt. "What makes you think it's a woman? Maybe I've developed a grand passion for gambling. No, Matt, I did not tell you her name." Then he laughed again. "Well, as a matter of fact, she is from back East after a fashion. She's a librarian from a small town in Wisconsin. You heard me correctly, I said she was a lady librarian from Wisconsin. Her name is Mary Beth Williams. Yes, I know it's about time. Look, little brother, I'm late to meet the lady as it is. I've got to go now. Just hold the fort on that Devens case until I get back. Thanks, Matt, you won't regret it."

Nick quickly hung up the telephone and picked up the pale blue silk tie from the bed and drew it around his neck. He tried to take it through the familiar motions, but he was suddenly all thumbs. He swore softly under his breath and tried again.

He was almost twenty minutes late when he stepped off the elevator into the lobby of the Golden Nugget Hotel. He wondered what Mary Beth's mood would be when she saw him. He was surprised, pleasantly so, to find that it was primarily one of relief. Her face lit up guilelessly the instant she spotted him.

"I'm sorry, sweetheart," he apologized, taking her hand in his and dropping a light kiss on her mouth. "I got tied up on a telephone call with my brother, Matt. We had a couple of cases he needed to discuss with me."

"It's all right." Mary Beth kept her voice casual and light. "I've been wondering how you can afford to take this much time off as it is."

"I can't afford not to." Nick did not expound. "You look stunning," he said appreciatively, his eyes darkening for an instant. "That dress must have cost you an arm and a leg."

"Several, actually," laughed Mary Beth.

"I didn't realize a librarian made that kind of money," he said softly, steadily.

"They don't." She'd been wanting to set the record straight for a week now, and this seemed to be the perfect opportunity. "But after Jeffrey made such a fool of himself by running off with a married woman, I decided whatever money was left from the cancelled wedding would only go for totally capricious things. So..." Mary Beth did a pirouette in the elegant black dress, sending the taffeta ruffles into a dark swirl around her body.

"Jeffrey was obviously a complete and utter fool, at best. But his loss is my gain. Some day I must thank him for that." Then Nick took her elbow and escorted her through the heavy brass doors into the warm summer night. "Let's grab a taxi here."

"Where are we going?"

"I made reservations for us at André's on South Sixth Street. I haven't eaten there before, but André's has the reputation of being one of the finest restaurants in the city," he explained as he handed her into the waiting taxi cab.

"What a lovely place," Mary Beth murmured as they drew up at the entrance of André's.

"It's a dream come true for the owner who renovated a private home of Spanish colonial design, originally built in the late 1920's, I believe," Nick told her as they were ushered into the restaurant.

The French countryside atmosphere with half-timbered, beamed-ceiling dining rooms awaited them. A very French maître d' made sure they were comfortably settled with their menus before Nick went on, "As I understand it, the complete menu from breads to desserts is made on the premises from scratch. The cuisine is basically French as you can see." He arched a dark brow. "I hope you like French cuisine."

Mary Beth smiled at him confidently. "I'm sure I will."

"Well, there's Veal *française*, and Scampi *provençale* if you like veal or shrimp." Nick studied the menu for a moment. "If you like seafood, there's the *Boudin aux fruits de mer*. That's a seafood 'sausage' of minced fresh sole, scallops, shrimp and crab. If you'd like something a bit more exotic, there's quails *en croûte* with sauce *le périgourdine*. And soufflé Grand Marnier, or perhaps a slice of French Silk pie to top it off."

"It all sounds delicious. But I think I'll have the Veal *française*," she told him when the waiter was ready to take their order. "How did you ever learn about this place?" she asked, her curiosity aroused.

Nick was very straightforward with her. "The same way I found out about Las Vegas the first time I came here. I read a lot and I asked a lot of questions."

Mary Beth gazed around the restaurant. "It is utterly charming." Then she sighed. "My father used to take me to places like this."

Nick selected a fine French vintage from the wine list and informed the steward of his choice before commenting, "Used to?"

"My father lives in Chicago now, but he travels a lot."

"With his fourth wife."

"Yes, with his fourth wife. He's a salesman of sorts, a kind of public relations representative with a nationally franchised travel agency." She unconsciously toyed with the delicate, argentine chain she wore about her neck. "Gerald is a very handsome, very charming man. I'm sure he's well-suited for that type of work." God knows he wasn't suited for much else in her opinion. But this was one time Mary Beth decided it would be wise to keep her opinions to herself.

A tentative smile crossed the man's face. "What about your mother? Somehow I imagine you're very much like her."

"I'd like to think I am. I hope that I am." Mary Beth stared down into the elegant glass of Bordeaux she was balancing between her fingertips. "My mother died when I was a teenager, Nick." She looked up at him, her eyes clear now. "I not only loved my mother very much, but I admired her. She was strong and intelligent. She was the best that a woman can be."

"And your father hasn't been the best that a man can be, is that it?" he ventured in a moment of unexpected insight.

"As I said, my father is a very handsome man. Handsome, but utterly irresponsible. He's never really grown up, even yet." Mary Beth took a sip of her wine and let the silence between them mature.

"So you're suspicious when it comes to men, especially good-looking men," said Nick, his handsome face taking on a judicial, appraising look.

She stiffened at the implied criticism. "Can you blame me?"

"In part, I can," he answered without a trace of his earlier humor. "It sounds to me like you've allowed your father and that one-time jackass fiancé of yours to do a job on you, sweetheart." Nick knew he'd come close to the truth, perhaps too close for Mary Beth's comfort. God knows, facing the harsh, unadorned truth about ourselves was often painful. He attempted a conciliatory smile. "Of course it's part of my business to look for ulterior motives. I'm afraid it's become a habit of mine. A bad habit at that."

"No. No, I think perhaps you're right," Mary Beth admitted reluctantly, turning her head to gaze vaguely out the window beside their table. She watched as the desert sun slipped behind a distant mountain.

It was Nick's deep voice reaching out to her that drew her back from the past. "Do you still believe in love, Mary Beth?"

She turned to face him. It was some moments before she was prepared to answer his question. "I don't know, Nick." And that was the unadorned truth. "Do you?"

"Yes, I believe in love." His voice was full and strong and utterly convincing. And in that instant, Mary Beth knew that Nick Durand was one hell of a good lawyer. "I believe that a man can love one woman all of his life," he continued. "If he's lucky enough to find the right woman."

"I used to believe in true love," she volunteered, "but when I look at men like Jeffrey, men like my father, then I confess that I just don't know anymore."

Nick leaned across the table and took her hand in his. The contrast between his larger, deeply-tanned fingers and hers stood out starkly against the pristine white tablecloth. "Jeffrey wasn't the right man for you, honey, and you weren't the right woman for him. Thank God. From what you've told me about your father, I'd venture to say that the whole problem is he's still in love with your mother, with the memory of your mother, and he doesn't know what to do about it."

Mary Beth's eyes grew darker and brimmed for a moment with two silvery teardrops. "Do you really think so? After all these years?"

Nick nodded emphatically. "Yes, even after all these years. Love doesn't end just because life has."

"I don't know why or how, but somehow, in some way, I know that you're right, Nicholas Durand." She gave his hand a little squeeze. "Thank you." She blinked several more times. "But that's enough about my family for one evening. Why don't you tell me more about yours?"

He seemed perfectly willing. "You've heard me talk about my younger brother, Matt. He's thirty and has been happily married to Kit for three years. They're expecting their first child sometime around Thanksgiving." He laughed joyously. "My parents are beside themselves with excitement. It will be their first grandchild. Anyway, Matt and I are partners in the law firm of Durand and Durand, which was founded by our grandfather back at the turn of the century. My parents and my grandparents and a slew of aunts and uncles and cousins and relations of every shape and size all live up around Elko County." He chuckled in the back of his throat. "We like to think of it as Durand country."

Mary Beth laughed with him. "Oh how lucky you are! I love big families. I've missed that so much since my mother and my grandparents passed away. With Gerald gone most of the time, there hasn't been much family life for the past few years." She looked at the man with eyes glistening with enthusiasm. "You mentioned a sister."

Nick nodded his head, then waited as their dinner was served. They agreed the food and the service were superb before continuing with their conversation.

"My sister, Meg, is only twenty-seven. She's the same age as you are, as a matter of fact. Meg was always the one with the wanderlust," said Nick affectionately. "She studied Romance languages at Stanford and married an up-and-coming young diplomat last year and off they went. They're currently assigned to the American embassy in Paris. And Meg is as happy in her way, halfway around the world, as Matt is in his simply to stay at home."

"And what about you, Nick?" Mary Beth asked. "Are you a homebody, too? Or do you dream of roaming the seven seas?"

He gave it careful consideration. "I love to travel, but I'm always ready to come home in the end. I guess I'm somewhere in between."

Mary Beth savored the last delectable bite of her veal, placed her fork on the plate in front of her, and then sat back a little in her chair.

"Everything in moderation, right?" She smiled at him.

"Right. Take gambling, for instance. Before anyone comes to Las Vegas, they should know how much money they can afford to lose. I always set a daily limit. That's how much I gamble with. If I were foolish enough to lose all of my money by lunchtime, then I'd be done gambling for the day. I don't believe that gambling is inherently immoral, but the consequences can be devastating if the person gambling doesn't have any self-control." He took a drink of his coffee. "And I don't think legalized gambling here in Nevada is much different than the kinds of gambling that go on in other states under any number of guises. In a sense, state lotteries and football pools and church bingo games can do the same damage. If someone wants to bet, there's always someone else there to take that bet." His dark brows formed a thoughtful line. "When you think about it, life's a gamble we all have to take if we want to win in the end."

Mary Beth found herself squirming uncomfortably under his intent gaze. "Is that meant as some kind of warning to me, Mr. Durand?"

Nick shook his head absently. "I was just wondering how much you'd be willing to risk in the name of love," he said in a deceptively mild tone.

She was a little shaken, and it showed. "As you know, I'm not much of a gambler."

· Nick seemed to shake off the mood that had held him momentarily in its grip. "Then why don't we go back to the Golden Nugget and play our lucky Keno numbers? We always said we would, and we haven't done it yet."

Mary Beth was visibly relieved. "Yes, let's! And thank you for the lovely dinner, Nick," she murmured graciously as they left André's and caught a cab back to downtown Las Vegas.

"It was my pleasure," replied Nick, slipping an arm around her shoulders and moving a little closer. "Do you think you can remember what our lucky numbers were?"

"Let me see..." She tried valiantly to ignore the man's sweet, hot breath as it wafted across her partially bare shoulder and arm, stirring the fine hairs there, caressing her skin like the whisper of the desert wind. Breathing was no longer automatic; she had to force the air in and out of her lungs. "I know the first two numbers were our ages, twenty-seven and thirty-two."

That was as far as Mary Beth got before she lost her concentration altogether. Her eyes closed involuntarily. She could almost feel the touch of his mouth, hot and feverish, on her bare flesh; his hands lingering over every nuance of her response, stroking her from shoulder to thigh, finding unerringly each and every secret spot as if he possessed a map of her vulnerabilities.

A shiver ran down the length of her body. Was Nick playing some kind of game with her? Her eyes flew open. He hadn't moved. He was still on his side of the cab exactly where she'd left him. It had all been a figment of her overactive imagination. Mary Beth blew out her breath expressively. And she had thought dancing with him was erotic. She didn't know the half of it!

"If I remember correctly we also used our birthdays," Nick contributed. "That gave us three, fifteen, ten and thirteen."

Mary Beth nodded. Her throat was constricted, but she managed to add, "And we met on the sixteenth."

"That's right, sixteen was on the list. Then there were your father's four wives and my two siblings—"

"'And a partridge in a pear tree,'" she sang softly under her breath.

Nick laughed out loud and pulled her closer. He looked down into her face and saw something there that stopped his laughter cold. "Mary Beth, what is it?" he demanded in a rapid, deep, unnatural voice.

But she was very much afraid that he knew precisely what it was that he saw in her eyes and on her lips and in her heart. It was her desire for him.

She turned into the crook of his shoulder, burying her face in the soft, richly textured material of his suit coat. Her voice was a mere whisper. "Oh God, Nick, I wish you would kiss me!"

He groaned and pressed closer still, the outline of his vibrant male form imprinting itself alongside hers. He made a frustrated sound in the back of his throat.

"I adore you, sweetheart, God knows I adore you, but your timing is lousy."

"I know, I know," she murmured feelingly as the taxi cab pulled up at the brightly lit front entrance of the Golden Nugget.

Nick quickly paid the cabbie off, stuffing some bills into the man's outstretched hand. Then he grasped Mary Beth firmly by the elbow and pulled her unceremoniously along the sidewalk until he found a darkened corner halfway down the city block.

He drew her into the protected niche and blocked out the rest of the world with his broad shoulders. "Would you like to repeat that wish now, Miss Williams?"

Mary Beth wrapped her fingers around the lapels of his jacket, and gazed up into his handsome face. "I wish you would kiss me, Nick."

"Oh Lord, and we've been so good all week!" the man moaned as he bent his head toward hers.

"Yes, we've been so good," Mary Beth whispered as she stood on tiptoe and entwined her arms tenaciously around his neck. "We've been so very good!"

Then their mouths came together and the world disintegrated around them. It all came apart: every good intention, every carefully maintained distance, every wild, impassioned kiss and stolen caress not carried through to its natural conclusion, every thought, every desire held in check. It all came crumbling down around them.

"Oh babe, what am I going to do with you?" muttered Nick, tearing his mouth from hers, resting his forehead against hers, his eyes closing in utter defeat, utter frustration.

"Hold me. Kiss me. Touch me, Nick. Let me hold and kiss and touch you," she told him in simple words. Then she felt the tremor that raced down his body.

"You're the only thing that could make me shiver on a hot summer night like tonight," he confessed, cupping her face between his hands, his thumbs stroking gently, insistently, at the corners of her mouth, urging her lips to open to his kiss.

Then he was devouring her with his lips and his teeth and his tongue. And Mary Beth discovered that there was nothing more seductive than knowing that a man wants a woman. Nick's desire for her was contagious. It was a wonderful, vicious circle of desire begetting desire begetting desire until it came full circle.

This was her moment. She felt, indeed, she believed herself to be the most desirable woman on the face of the earth. That was the magic of his touch. That was the incomparable gift that Nick gave to her. And she gave him back in kind by responding to his kiss, to his caress, as if she felt it and knew it for what it was all in that one instant: her life's blood. She wanted his mouth on her, his hands, his tongue, in ways she had scarcely dared to imagine.

There was a core of sensuality to her that she was only now beginning to acknowledge and understand. She was a sentient, physical creature. Her head did not always rule her body.

She could taste the man in her very soul as his tongue swept into her mouth, sizzling hot and molasses-sweet on a lazy, love-heated summer night. His fingernail scraped her nipple through the layer of black taffeta, and she felt the tiny earthquake along the entire length of her body. His touch, his kiss tore her apart, then put her back together again.

She leaned into him, clung to him, her fingers digging into the hard flesh at his waist. His breathing was rough, shallow. She could feel his chest rise and fall in rapid succession. And she could feel the undeniable force of his erection. It was there, between them, an earthy, fundamental reminder that they were only human.

It was a sharp, shrill chorus of wolf whistles, followed by mocking, suggestive laughter, that finally drove them apart. Two young men, dressed in faded jeans and T-shirts, swaggered on by them. One let out with another low whistle as they passed.

Nick muttered an unintelligible oath or two under his breath that were, in Mary Beth's estimation, best left unintelligible. She was embarrassed enough as it was.

"I'm sorry, Mary Beth. I don't know what got into me." Nick denied this with a shake of his head. "I don't normally get carried away like that on a public street."

She experienced a brittle sense of calm, made all the more incredible when she acknowledged that her body had just melted all over the man like thick, sweet honey left in the sun. There was danger here. She saw it. She felt it. And yet she still rushed to meet it. She was, it seemed, as weak and as silly as the next woman when it came to a pair of broad shoulders and a lean waist and taut thighs filled with masculine promise. She was a fool.

"I—I think we'd better go inside," she mumbled, her tongue thick in her mouth.

"In a minute. We'll go inside in a minute," Nick advised with an ironic smile that spoke of the inevitable vulnerability of the male physique. He made no attempt to move.

Mary Beth pushed her hair back off her face, determined not to blush or pull away like some kind of adolescent schoolgirl. The soft, golden-brown curls at her temples were slightly damp. "Whew, its warm tonight!" she exclaimed, fanning herself with one hand. "I think I'll order a frozen daiquiri while we play our Keno numbers."

"I think I'll order a nice cold shower," muttered Nick as he finally moved away from her. Mary Beth couldn't help the little burst of laughter that escaped her. "Well, it's damned awkward, that's what it is!" he growled. "You women have it lucky."

"Do we?"

"Yes, you don't wear your heart on your sleeve, metaphorically speaking."

Mary Beth's eyes grew wide. "Nicholas James Durand, are you trying to tell me that you're embarrassed by what happened back there?"

"Yes. Yes, I am," he admitted as they strolled along the street toward the Golden Nugget. "I don't mind if you know I want you. I couldn't help that even if I wanted to." Now it was Mary Beth's turn to be embarrassed. "But I thought I had more control over myself than to allow it to happen on a main public thoroughfare, for God's sake. I'm not a hot-blooded kid anymore, honey. I'm thirty-two years old and I ought to know better by now." Nick shook his head, befuddled. "I just don't understand it."

Mary Beth patted his arm solicitously and blurted out, "Let's just chalk it up to my irresistible charms and let it go at that."

She saw a sudden flash of teeth. "Maybe you're right. Maybe it is your irresistible charms, as you so delicately put it," he agreed with a slightly wicked grin. Then he shrugged his broad, eloquent shoulders. "I guess I'm just putty in your hands, darling."

"Oh, sure." She shot him a quelling glance and he laughed.

"I thought you said these were supposed to be our 'lucky' numbers," Mary Beth was double-checking with him nearly an hour and two frozen daiquiris later. "We haven't won a thing."

Nick's face relaxed into an indulgent smile. "How much have we lost?"

Mary Beth wrinkled her brow. "No more than a few dollars, I would guess."

"Believe me, in Las Vegas that's considered winning," Nick drawled as he picked up a black crayon and marked their next ticket. "Remember what I told you about the game of Keno that first night we played here?" he reminded her diplomatically.

"Yes, I remember. You told me that Keno was a good way to rest your weary feet, have a cool drink and lose your money in pleasant surroundings," she sighed, taking a sip of her daiquiri. "Or words to that effect, anyway. I don't suppose we can expect much more than than out of life sometimes."

"I'm afraid our lucky numbers have lost again," he announced at the conclusion of the next game.

"Although I'm up several hundred dollars for the week, I'm down to my last ten dollars of gambling money for the day," Mary Beth said, making a little face.

Nick dove into his suit pocket. "And here's my last ten of today's allowance. Why don't we pool our resources and give the dollar slot machines a whirl?"

"Why not?" she agreed, brightening.

Nick got to his feet and held his hand out to her invitingly. "We'll make it a true joint venture. You can supply the brains by choosing the machine and putting the money in the slot, and I'll supply the brawn by pulling the handle."

"And who says men don't serve their purpose?" Mary Beth laughed, amused by her own witticism. She noticed, however, that Nick chose to ignore her comment.

They made their way through the usual Friday night crowd and located an area of one-dollar slot machines on the far side of the casino. Nick exchanged their twenty dollars for twenty playing tokens, while Mary Beth reached out and touched the colorful surface of the first open slot machine they came to. Then she shook her head and moved on to the next. Again she shook her head and moved on.

"What the devil are you doing?" Nick finally inquired.

"You said I could choose the slot machine, and that's exactly what I'm doing. I'm trying to get a feel for one of these. I just know our lucky slot machine is here if we can just find it."

Nick laughed outright and dropped a light kiss on her mouth. "You should see your face, sweetheart."

"Why? What's wrong with it?"

"Nothing." His eyes had gone very dark and his voice was a little husky. "You look just like a kid on Christmas morning with a passel of pretty packages to unwrap."

"Let's try this one," she suggested, stopping in front of a deluxe one-armed bandit with a shiny chromium finish and glowing neon lights. "We can win on cherries and oranges and plums and melons and bells and sevens—"

"And the odds are against us winning on anything, you know that," Nick responded. "I don't want to spoil your fun, honey, but the odds of winning playing the slots are higher than just about any other game in Vegas."

"I know that," she said, unruffled. "But it's like those contests that come in the mail all the time back home. I figure someone somewhere has to win sometime."

Nick stood there, shaking his head. He had to admit it was impossible to argue with that kind of logic. "To cover all the winning combinations on this particular machine, you'll need to put in three coins."

"All right, here we go!" Mary Beth alerted him. She dropped three coins into the slot, one by one, and then motioned for him to pull the handle. The reels spun around and around and when they finally stopped, one lone cherry symbol popped up on the face of the machine. Then two coins dropped noisily into the tray at the bottom. "See, we won!" she exclaimed. "I knew this was going to be our lucky slot machine."

Nick wasn't sure how she figured they'd won when the machine took three coins and only gave back two in return, but he wouldn't dream of raining on her parade. "Do you want to try again?"

Mary Beth looked up at him, her eyes aglow with excitement. "Of course. Don't you?"

He nodded, and she dropped three more coins down the throat of the hungry machine. He pulled the handle and the reels spun and a plum and an orange and a bell all came up, but nothing dropped into the tray this time.

"C'mon, Lady Luck, where are you?" muttered Mary Beth as she quickly reloaded the one-armed bandit.

They played again and again, sometimes winning two, or even five coins, before the machine inevitably reclaimed them.

"We're down to our last six dollars, Nick," she informed the man at long last.

"You may as well put them in too, honey, and then we'll call it a night," he suggested, stifling a yawn.

Mary Beth took a deep breath and put in three of the six remaining coins she held in her open palm. "Here goes."

On cue, Nick gave the handle a vigorous pull. The reels spun around and around until the first one came to a stop. A seven popped up on the face of the slot machine. And then another seven, and finally a third seven.

"Well, I'll be a son of a—" Nick's voice was drowned out by the loud bells that started to ring and the metallic din of coins shooting out into the tray. A bright red light on the top of the one-armed bandit began to flash.

Mary Beth sank her fingers into his arms, her eyes huge and uncertain. "What is it? What's happened?" she demanded to know.

"What's happened?" Nick Durand put his head back and laughed. "What's happened is that we've won!" he shouted over the pandemonium.

"We've won?" Mary Beth shouted back.

"Yes, we've won the super jackpot!" Nick pointed his finger at her. "You and me, sweetheart. We've just won five thousand dollars!"

Five

Five thousand dollars!

Mary Beth stared up into Nick's eyes. She couldn't believe it! Her mouth opened, the words formed on her lips, but no sound came out. She snapped her mouth shut, then opened it again. Laughter bubbled up out of her throat. "Five thousand dollars? How? Why?"

"How? Simple. We came up with three lovely little sevens all in a row," he explained in a voice that carried over the noise of the crowd. "Why? Because like I told you before, sweetheart, we're good luck for each other." Then Nick bent his head and kissed her soundly on the lips.

Mary Beth could feel the excitement and the sexual tension searing the air between them like heat lightning on a hot summer night. It was there just beneath the surface of their otherwise civilized behavior. It was like a shot of pure adrenaline to the system. The blood was pounding in their veins. Their hearts were racing. It wouldn't take much. It wouldn't take much at all, she secretly admitted as they pulled away from each other.

Nick raised his head reluctantly. *Whoa, boy*. This isn't the time or the place, he reminded himself. Over Mary Beth's shoulder he spotted a casino official and a guard coming toward them through the crowd; a crowd that always seemed to gather at the first sign of excitement.

"Congratulations on winning the five-thousand-dollar jackpot, folks," said a distinguished-looking man as he extended his hand, first to Mary Beth and then to Nick. "I'm Mr. White of the Golden Nugget staff."

"I'm Nick Durand and this is Mary Beth Williams." Nick took care of the introductions on their side.

The guard took a set of keys that hung from a large ring on his belt and did something to the slot machine that shut off the ringing bells and the flashing lights as the last few coins spewed into the tray.

"As you may know already, this machine will only pay out two hundred dollars of your super jackpot. If you would like to collect that now, we'll make sure you receive the balance due to you. We'll also need some information, including your social security numbers, for the Internal Revenue Service. If you will follow me, please. It's this way," the man said, once Nick and

Mary Beth had scooped the coins into one of the large plastic buckets provided for just such an occasion.

"I still can't believe it." Mary Beth was laughing giddily under her breath as Nick took her arm and directed her toward the cashier's window. "Five thousand dollars! The odds of winning that much must be astronomical."

"I'm no mathematician, but I'd say you hit it right on the nose," Nick said as they supplied the cashier with their addresses and the other information required in exchange for the balance of their money.

"You may deposit all or part of your winnings with the cashier if you like," suggested Mr. White. "The casino provides the banking service as a security measure for those who prefer not to keep the money with them. If you have any other questions, please don't hesitate to ask."

"Thank you for your help, Mr. White," Nick said cordially as the man concluded his business with them. "Listen, honey, the man has a good point. We don't want to be carrying that kind of cash around with us. I say we keep it right here in the casino vault," he told Mary Beth once the money had been counted out in stacks of one-hundred-dollar bills. "We can get it any time we want to."

"Yes, let's leave it in the vault," she quickly agreed. "I still can't believe the money's ours anyway."

"It is a little unbelievable, isn't it?" Nick said, shaking his head as they each signed a receipt for twenty-five hundred dollars. "It seems more like 'funny' money than real money," he concluded as he folded the receipt and slipped it into his wallet. "Now

I think we should do something to celebrate the occasion. Why don't we have a bottle of Dom Perignon sent up to my room?''

Whether it was the rather remarkable events of the evening, or her determination to live the fantasy to its fullest, Mary Beth never knew for sure. After all, it wasn't every day that a girl dressed in an expensive designer gown, dined on exquisite French cuisine and was swept off her feet by a handsome leading man. Not to mention the grand finale: winning a five-thousand-dollar jackpot. It could have been any or all of these things.

Or none of them.

In the end, Mary Beth only knew that she was attracted to Nick Durand as she had been attracted to no other man in her twenty-seven years. She only knew that she suddenly heard her own voice suggesting, "Let's have the champagne sent to my room. It's closer.''

It was scarcely a legitimate argument since her room was on the sixth floor of the hotel and Nick's was on the ninth. But neither of them was interested in belaboring the point.

One thing was clear. They wanted to be alone. For one solid week they had surrounded themselves with bright lights and loud music and other people, always other people. It had been deliberate, of course. They'd both recognized the dangers of being together and alone. Now they wanted to be alone, just the two of them.

Nick picked up a house phone in the lobby and placed their order for room service even before they took an elevator for the sixth floor. They spoke little on the short elevator ride, and not at all as Mary Beth took out her room key and unlocked the door. After a week of avoiding each other's hotel rooms like the plague, it seemed awkward to try to make themselves feel at home now.

Mary Beth began to chat about anything and everything that came to mind as she moved nervously about the room. She switched on the lights and straightened the morning newspapers she had left scattered across the desk, trying to make conversation with a man she'd always felt so comfortable talking to—until this very moment.

"I still can't believe we won five thousand dollars, Nick. Do you believe it? And to think we were nearly ready to give up and call it a night. We only had enough money for one more round and that would have been it. I didn't know what to think when that red light started flashing and those bells starting going off. I wasn't sure what was happening." Mary Beth came to a dead stop. She had literally run out of breath. It was only then she realized that she'd been forgetting to breathe.

She just wasn't any good at this, she decided, as she finally came to rest somewhere in the region of the red velvet settee. She stood there with one hand on the back of the cushioned sofa. The other one pulled the drapes back so she could look out at the sea of lights below, a stream of neon color that stretched to the horizon. Glitter Gulch, isn't that what they called this part of town?

Nick came up and stood behind her, silent and strong. She could feel his presence. He emanated a masculine heat and a distinctive male scent that was unmistakable in the cool, air-conditioned room. Then she felt his hands drop lightly onto her shoulders.

"You're as nervous as a high-strung filly, sweetheart. Would you prefer I leave?"

So, he knew. He knew of her unspoken fears, her insecurities, her terrible indecisiveness now that they were finally alone. He knew. She should have known he would.

Oh God, what did a woman do with a man who knew her secrets? What did she do with a man who knew all about her fears and her fantasies and her dreams? Suddenly, Mary Beth felt vulnerable. Exposed. Naked.

"No, don't leave, Nick. Stay. The champagne will be here soon. Please, stay." It didn't even sound like her voice.

The tension in the room was so thick it could have been sliced with a knife. It shattered when a knock came at the door.

"Room service, sir," announced the uniformed waiter as he wheeled the cart into the center of the deep-piled red carpet. Then he expertly removed the cork, returning the bottle of champagne to the ice bucket at Nick's polite insistence. "Thank you, sir. I hope you and the lady enjoy your champagne," he said as he slipped Nick's generous tip into his pants' pocket and left.

Nick poured two glasses of the pale champagne as Mary Beth walked across the room toward him. But he never handed her the glass. They never drank the champagne.

Something inside Nick snapped when Mary Beth came up to him like that with her hand outstretched. She was a vision in the chic, strapless gown. Her milky-white skin contrasted startlingly with the blue-black taffeta.

Oh what a temptation to see if the milky-white skin extended beneath the fitted bodice! What an unholy temptation to unhook the back of her dress and pull the zipper down and have her breasts spill into his hands, to see and feel their hardening arousal, to taste their lacteal sweetness.

Instead of handing her the glass of champagne, Nick set both glasses down on the cart again and opened his arms to her. It was a simple gesture. An invitation. An invitation she accepted.

Mary Beth went to him without a sound, without a moment's hesitation. Their arms went around each other. They stood there, holding one another, looking into each other's eyes.

Nick wrapped his arms tightly around her, bringing her up against the full length of his body. The taffeta ruffles were caught between them, crushed against the fine fabric of his suit. And neither of them cared.

"I wish I could sweep you off your feet," he drawled, his mouth taking loving little bites of her delicately shaped ears, the enticing curve where her neck met bare shoulder, the soft swell of her breasts above the contrasting dark gown.

"You can, Nick. You can sweep me off my feet with just one look, one kiss," she confessed.

He did not bother to disguise his pleasure at her words. He kissed her for a long time before he breathed into her mouth, "I want to make love to you, Mary Beth Williams. I have since that first night when I took you into my arms and we danced in the dark. Does that frighten you?"

"A little," she whispered. "No, Nick. No, don't pull away. If I were to take all the bits and pieces of my dreams about the man I would most want to make love with, it would be you, Nicholas James Durand. It would be you," she admitted, laying her heart bare. "You must know that you are the man of my fantasies, the man of my dreams."

For the space of a heartbeat or two, Nick was very still. Then he caught his breath, it sounded like a groan. "Mary Beth, how could I even think to question what you would be willing to risk in the name of love? You're so sweet, so damned sweet, and so open to me, honey."

Then he buried his face in her hair; it was warm and soft and sweet-smelling. His hands moved up and down her body, lingering, enjoying, arousing her with his touch. And, in turn, he too was aroused. He could feel her legs tremble revealingly against his. He cupped her rounded bottom in his palms and deliberately brought her into the enclave of his thighs. He massaged the small of her back until she instinctively arched into him. It was torture of the very sweetest kind.

Mary Beth felt her hands reach out for him. Her nails lightly raked across his chest, creating a tiny trail of goose bumps right through the smooth material of his dress shirt. She grasped him about the waist and held on for dear life when his caress drew a moan of pleasure from her lips. She could no more disguise her passionate response to him than he could deny his physical reaction to her. His body grew bold and insistent. She was melting.

"I don't understand what's happening between us, Nick," she cried out softly.

"I can't say that I understand either, darling." He shook his head as he held her almost reverently in his hands. "But just because we don't understand it, doesn't make it any less real, does it?"

"No, it doesn't make it any less real," Mary Beth agreed in a whisper as he undid the back of her gown and eased the zipper down.

Nick slid the bodice of her dress down around her waist. The lacy bandeau beneath was next. He unhooked it and tossed it on the bed without a second thought. Then her breasts were bared and Nick couldn't seem to keep his eyes off her. They rode high and firm on her rib cage. They were proud and milky-white, silky and smooth as satin, with rose-red, impertinent tips that eagerly grew and hardened under his intent study. "Yes, we're attracted to each other, damned attracted. And that's the truth."

Mary Beth couldn't seem to breathe for a moment. Was it the unadorned truth of his words, or his touch on her flesh? "And your whole life is dedicated to the pursuit of truth, isn't it?" she challenged, breathless.

Nick's eyes, dark as the desert night, looked down into hers. "Yes, it is. Truth as I see it. Truth as I believe it to be," he stated with rock-solid conviction.

"But truth, even the truth of the law, is anything but a simple matter of black and white."

She dared to go one step further. "And what is the truth about you and me, Nick?"

"We're a man and woman strongly attracted to each other," he growled in a low-pitched rumble. "We may be falling in love."

Mary Beth had to know that much for sure. "And that is the truth as you see it?" she demanded softly, insistently.

"Yes," Nick pledged. "Now I promise we're going to relax and take this one step at a time, sweetheart," he murmured, bending his head to kiss her nipple.

She could feel the moist heat of his mouth on her, the hard, arrowed tip of his tongue tracing an erotic pattern back and forth across the rigid tip of her breast, the edges of his teeth nipping that most sensitive, womanly flesh. Her pulse began to beat in double time. First her heart was in her throat, then it seemed to tumble all the way down to her feet. She found her hands clasping his head, her fingers entwining in his hair, her head thrown back as a low, impassioned moan rushed past her parted lips.

Nick sank to his knees in front of her, burying his head in the natural cradle of her hips. She was bursting into flames in his arms. He could feel the heat pouring from her body. He knew that her skin must be tinged with pink, her body soft and moist. Her breathing was shallow and erratic. She was aroused, and he discovered that the thought aroused him as well.

He was aroused to the point where he felt his self-control slipping away from him. His need for her was elemental; his desire for her indisputable. He felt as though he would explode at the slightest provocation. He could never remember being so aroused. The realization left him stunned, shaken to the core.

"Nick. Come here, darling," she beckoned then in a voice that snatched the breath out of his lungs. He rose to his feet, automatically. He gazed down into Mary Beth's eyes and found them all soft and smoky. "I want to know what love is, Nick. What it is to be loved by you."

His intense gaze burned her. "And I want to know what it is to love you, Mary Beth, and to be loved by you."

Then his parted lips were on hers, hungrily, a little harshly, and his tongue was buried deep inside her mouth. She wanted to take him into her. She could almost imagine what it would be like to be truly and fully possessed by this man.

Her breasts ached for his touch. Her nipples were almost painfully aroused as they brushed across the front of his shirt. She wanted desperately to feel her bare skin against him. She wanted to rub against him and feel the delicious, erotic tickle of his chest hair on her sensitized flesh. Yet she was self-conscious about standing there half-undressed while Nick was fully clothed. Still, to suggest that he take his clothes off was beyond Mary Beth at this point.

Passion found a way where courage had failed. She began to fumble with the buttons down his shirt-front. When she finally had every last one undone, she pulled the material free of his trousers. Then she reached down and unbuttoned first one sleeve and then the other, so that Nick could shrug the shirt off altogether and toss it on the nearest chair.

Now they were both nude to the waist, and the feel of him as she rubbed up against him, the myriad sensations that flooded her mind and her body as he lightly stroked her, left Mary Beth purring like a cat.

"Let me finish undressing you, sweetheart," Nick said in a tightly controlled voice as he tore himself away from her.

He eased the designer gown down over her hips until it was no more than a puddle of midnight-black around her feet. He bent and picked up the dress and hung it carefully over the same chair where he'd tossed his shirt. Then he pulled her high-heeled sandals and silk stockings off and quickly dispensed with them, leaving her standing in only a pair of lacy bikini panties. He took a step back and stared at her long and hard, his eyes as dark as Mary Beth had ever seen them. She was nearly tempted to grab for her clothes, for the bedspread, for anything to cover herself.

"Nick?" Surely he must realize how uncomfortable he was making her feel.

"My God, but you're lovely!" The words shot out of his mouth. He took a step toward her. "You're the loveliest thing I've ever seen, Mary Beth. Don't you know that?"

"No." She shook her head, the color high on her cheeks. She resisted the urge to fold her arms modestly across her breasts.

"There's no need to be shy with me, sweetheart," he reassured her. "You're perfect, perfect to look at, perfect to touch, perfect to love."

Nick kicked his shoes off as his hands went to the belt buckle at his waist. Without one bit of the self-consciousness she was experiencing, he stepped out of his clothes and stood before her.

"You're beautiful!" Mary Beth blurted out. Nick flushed an attractive shade of crimson. "I'm sorry," she stammered. "I didn't mean to embarrass you."

"Hell, you really didn't embarrass me, honey. It's just that the only person who's ever called me beautiful before is my mother. And I understand that I wasn't very old at the time," Nick told her, his voice a throaty rumble.

"Well, you are beautiful," she vowed, taking a step toward him, drawn to him. "I've seen statues of beautiful men, even great paintings of beautiful men, but I've never seen a beautiful man of flesh and blood."

She reached out with a tentative, solitary finger and touched him. It was a mere whisper, a mere promise of a touch, first to a muscular arm, then to his chest and lower to the smooth, taut abdomen, still lower to the line of his hip and the sinewy musculature of his thigh. Mary Beth made no secret of it; she found his body fascinating. Endlessly fascinating.

Then she touched him again, intimately, and she heard Nick's sharp intake of air. His body responded immediately as she half-hoped, half-feared it would. A surge of feminine power flowed through her as surely as the raw power that surged into his body. Her hand closed around him, gently but firmly. His very strength, indeed, his greatest vulnerability, was now within her velvet grasp. She felt victorious, triumphant, and scared to death.

"Nick—?" It was a little cry for help.

But he seemed to be having difficulty breathing, not to mention speaking. There were small beads of perspiration on his forehead. "It's all right, darling. Believe me, you're doing fine. Just fine," he assured her huskily. Then he reached down and gently released her fingers and took her hand in his. "Come to bed with me now, Mary Beth. Come to bed," he urged, pushing the discarded bandeau aside and pulling back the velvet bedspread.

Seduced by his words and by his passion for her, Mary Beth moved toward the bed. She slipped between the sheets while Nick turned off a light, leaving the shaded floor lamp glowing in the corner. There were Victorian reproduction lamps turned down low on the bedside tables.

Then he was slipping into the king-size bed beside her, taking her into his arms, his sheer, unrestrained strength holding her as surely as any golden chains.

How right, how natural it seemed to go to this man, Mary Beth thought. They'd laughed together, oh how they'd laughed together in the days past, and they'd shared a few tears, admittedly most of them hers. It seemed so right, so natural to be together now, making love.

"Talk to me, Mary Beth. Tell me how you feel. Tell me *what* you feel," Nick entreated, his lips moving over her face, his hands over her body.

"I feel like I've walked into a dream," she confessed, "into my own dream. I feel your weight on mine, your skin smooth and soft. I didn't think you would be so smooth and soft, Nick." Her hands slid down his passion-slick skin, surveying his body with meticulous care and a surprisingly open, erotic curiosity. "I feel your muscles sleek and hard. Your hair so fine," she murmured, curling a small bunch around her finger. "Your man's body is the ultimate paradox. Soft on the one hand, hard on the other. Smooth, yet rough. Strong, so strong, and yet so terribly vulnerable." His hands glided down her body and she could barely speak. "Now it's your turn. Tell me what you feel."

Nick looked intently into her eyes. "Lady, I feel...I feel your skin glow, warm and rich, like silk when I touch you. You're half afraid of me, and yet you want me as no other woman has. Buried somewhere deep inside you is a passionate woman, a woman ready to burst into white-hot flames if the right man loves her in the right way. I sense it. I feel it. I believe I'm that man for you." He lay there for a moment, and took in every lovely inch of her from her head to her toes. "I want our first time together to be so damned good for you, sweetheart. I want to know what you like and what you don't like."

"I don't know," Mary Beth whispered hoarsely. "I don't know."

"Then we'll find out together," Nick promised, kneeling over her, his muscular legs straddling her body.

He lowered his head, and she watched with utter fascination as he touched the tip of his tongue to the tip of her breast. He drew a moist circle around it, once, twice, three times. She lost count after that. He moved on to the other breast, then back and forth between them in agonizing slow motion until Mary Beth heard herself moan. Her breasts were throbbing with an almost painful need for his possession.

"Oh my God!" she cried out when she thought she couldn't bear it for an instant longer. "Help me, Nick!"

He raised his head. His face was flushed. His eyes were dark and glowing. "Do you like having your breasts touched? Do you like being caressed?"

"Yes! Yes, I like what you do to me. I love what you do to me."

Then he drew her nipple between his lips, first one and then the other, back and forth in a lazy, erotic pattern of nipping and teasing and cajoling, until Mary Beth only knew vaguely that her head was moving mindlessly from side to side on the pillow. If this was a dream, then she never wanted to awaken.

"I'm ready now, Nick. I'm ready now!" she gasped, aware of the heat penetrating her flesh, sensing the woman's essence that flowed from her body, compelling her to react.

"You think you are, darling, but give it time. Give it time. We have all the time in the world," he drawled, gazing down at her, that endearing, half-crooked smile of his on his handsome face. "Making love is so much more than rushing toward a climax. It's not the destination, sweetheart, it's the journey," Nick assured her, his fingers stroking her, soothing her, exciting her as they blazed a trail from the hollow at the base of her throat, down between the ivory silk of her breasts, across her abdomen, causing her to take in her breath sharply, before they descended to the very center of her woman's body. He gently parted her tender flesh, then delved deeper and deeper, finding her wet and warm and welcoming.

A slow burning started down deep inside her, somewhere she'd never been before. It burned warm at first, then the fire grew hotter and hotter. It spread in an ever-increasing circle until it engulfed her, until it threatened to consume her entirely. She perished in its white-hot flames and emerged on the other side: new, renewed, yet changed. Changed in a most wondrous way. Like the phoenix of ancient legend, she rose up out of the ashes, the ashes of her passion.

She wasn't at all the kind of human being she'd thought she was. She wasn't practical or sensible or controlled. She was wild and free and as natural as the heat of the desert under the burning sun and as cool as the desert night under a slice of pale desert moon. And it was their secret, hers and Nick's. Perhaps that was always the secret of lovers: to know each other as no one else does, to exist for those few stolen moments in a private world where no one else dare go. It was their secret, and Mary Beth took it to her heart and she kept it there.

When she could stand no more, his name became a litany on her lips. "Nick! Only you, Nick!"

"Yes, sweetheart, only you and only now. Now!" he grated through his teeth as he rose above her, his broad shoulders blocking all else but him from her view.

Then he was there, easing into her, surging into her, filling her body until she could no longer distinguish his flesh from her own. They were separate halves, yet one whole. They were male and female, made for each other, fitted perfectly one to the other, hard and soft, sleek and inviting, giving and taking.

He went into her and Mary Beth grasped him, enfolded him, urging him further and further into her loving warmth. It wasn't something she did intentionally, it was merely, miraculously, her body's natural response to his sensual invasion.

Then he began to move inside her, wondrously slowly, allowing her, forcing her to feel the raw power of his possession. When it came, the change in his movements was so subtle that Mary Beth scarcely realized it until he was thrusting again and again, deeper and deeper, each thrust of greater intensity than the one before it.

"I do want you, Nick," she gasped, "I do hunger for you. And I feel a little crazy"—she laughed breathlessly—"I am a little crazy."

"And I'm crazy about you, Mary Beth. Crazy about you!" Nick said in a low, vehement voice. Then his fingers were digging into her as he grasped her buttocks in his hands and cried out, "Now, sweetheart?"

"Yes, now, now!" she answered before her world stopped turning.

She was left floating, floating somewhere where she had no weight, no body, no mind. There was nothing but pure sensation. Sweet sensation. Sensations such as she had never known, never dreamed of, never fantasized about. Then she felt the pulsing release of Nick's body as he came into her, and she gloried in the knowledge, as women have since the beginning. She clung to him, her arms and legs wrapped around him, feeling his heartbeat racing on the desert wind with her own.

Then it was over.

But it would never truly be over, Mary Beth thought, bemused. It would always be there, tucked away inside her, hers to remember as long as she had a heart and a mind and a soul.

They drifted in and out of sleep for half the night, dozing in each other's arms, talking quietly and intimately, making love again when they could no longer resist the temptation. Then, with the golden flush of a new dawn breaking across the desert sky, they fell well and truly asleep at last.

The bright midday sun was pouring in the window between the velvet drapes when Mary Beth next awakened. She knew immediately where she was, and who was there alongside her. She stretched contentedly, aware of her body as she had never been before.

She felt good. In fact, she felt wonderful. A little sore in spots, but that was to be expected. It was a small price to pay for a night in Nick's arms, for a night in paradise.

"Good morning, sleepyhead," came his sleep-rusty, masculine voice from the pillow beside her. "How did you sleep?"

Mary Beth turned over into the welcoming circle of his arms. "Like a baby. How about you?" she asked, snuggling up to him.

"Hmm—" Nick brushed his chin back and forth along her bare shoulder, the abrasive stubble of his beard bringing her sleeping flesh to life "—best night's sleep I've had in years. Best of anything I've had in years," he laughed softly. He saw the flicker of challenge in her intelligent brown eyes and quickly amended his statement. "Making love with you last night was the best thing that's ever happened to me, sweetheart, and you damn well know it."

"Yes, I know," Mary Beth sniffed, her confidence rising. "I was simply wondering if you did."

Nick pushed himself up on the oversized pillow into a half-sitting position and clasped his hands behind his head. His brow creased thoughtfully for a moment, and his voice dropped to just above a whisper. "We were lucky last night, Mary Beth. You know that, don't you?"

She gazed up into his handsome face, deciding that she actually preferred him like this, with the rough beginnings of a beard on his chin and his hair all tousled and nothing more than a rumpled sheet modestly covering the lower half of his torso. She reluctantly tore her eyes away. "Yes, I know, we were lucky," she murmured.

Neither of them was talking about the five-thousand-dollar jackpot, but that was the direction their conversation took next.

"What are you going to do with your half of the money?" Nick inquired, his curiosity getting the best of him.

Mary Beth gave it about thirty seconds of thought before she answered. "I think I'd like to give part of it to the public library here in Las Vegas."

Nick nodded his head approvingly. "Commendable. Definitely commendable. And don't forget you have to put a chunk of it aside for dear old Uncle Sam," he reminded her. Then he snapped his fingers. "And I think we should go out and buy ourselves a souvenir of Las Vegas."

She sat up in bed beside him and pulled the sheet up under her arms. "Why don't we take part of the money and go out to the Strip this afternoon? I've heard there are some beautiful shops at Caesar's Palace and at the Hilton. I haven't seen as much of the famous Las Vegas Strip as I'd like to, anyway."

"We'll do whatever you want, sweetheart," Nick murmured, bending his head to nuzzle her neck.

"*Anything* I want?" said Mary Beth, experimenting with her newfound power over him.

"Anything," he promised, sliding down in the bed and pulling her with him.

"All right, then let's have breakfast," she suggested saucily. "I'm starved."

Nick grunted noncommittally and began to kiss her, raining a light erotic shower on her mouth, her eyes, the hollow at the base of her throat. All the while his hands were delving beneath the sheet, eliciting an involuntary response from her. His intent was unmistakable. "Whatever you say, lady," he drawled, unconcerned, tossing aside the bedcovers and moving to cover her with his body.

Mary Beth groaned and slipped her arms around him. There was no sense in trying to fight the inevitable, especially when the inevitable was so much to her liking. "Maybe we could have lunch," she breathed against his mouth. "A very late lunch..."

Six

It all began innocently enough that night at the Four Queens Casino. They were a few friendly tourists betting a dollar or two at the blackjack table, sipping a cup of coffee or a soft drink or a sloe gin fizz, and talking to each other as strangers do in Las Vegas. Mary Beth was in the seat to the dealer's far right. She would be the last one to play, the anchor man, as it was called in blackjack.

A short, stocky man with steel-gray hair and a military haircut was in the first seat. He'd told everyone when he sat down at the table that his name was Ralph Munser and he was here in Las Vegas with his wife, Evelyn. It was the Munsers' first vacation in twenty years. They were wheat farmers from Kansas, and there was little time for vacations when you were a wheat farmer.

Between Ralph and Mary Beth, there were two nurses from San Antonio, both redheads and in their mid-forties, and an elegantly dressed woman who introduced herself as Margaret Best. Margaret was one of those people who would never grow old. There was a sparkle in her blue eyes, and a youthful energy in the way she talked. She could have been anywhere between the ages of sixty and eighty. It was anyone's guess. She was with a tour group from Seattle, and she talked a lot about her four grandchildren.

The dealer was a personable young woman who wore a name tag identifying her as Jacki. Jacki had the most beautiful hands and fingernails that Mary Beth had ever seen. No doubt stock-in-trade here in Las Vegas.

The cards were shuffled, cut and replaced in the wooden shoe, and the next hand was dealt all around. Mary Beth picked up her cards and studied them for a moment. She was holding a king and a queen, two face cards. They added up to twenty. Not a bad hand, she deduced, slipping the cards under her chips.

Tonight she was wearing a cotton and silk blend sundress in a becoming shade of Chinese blue. There was a coordinating, oversized kerchief in a cream and blue pattern that tied around her shoulders. The outfit was something she'd bought that afternoon in a dress shop out on the Strip.

Mary Beth reached up and touched the necklace that sparkled against the hollow of her throat. It was a present from Nick. She smiled. They'd been a little crazy that afternoon picking out a souvenir of Las Vegas for each other at Nick's insistence. She'd finally bought him a Lady Luck tie tack done in tiny emeralds. He'd given her the necklace she was wearing. It spelled out Las Vegas in eighteen-karat gold letters and was punctuated above each *a* with a small, brilliant-cut diamond.

Not the kind of thing one usually wore to the monthly meeting of the Greensport Library Board, Mary Beth thought, nearly laughing out loud.

But then she wasn't in Greensport, Wisconsin. She was in Las Vegas, Nevada, and she was a different woman here. Or did it have less to do with where she was, and more to do with one very handsome, very charming man who'd swept her off her feet last night?

At the memory of last night—in fact, at the memory of that very morning—Mary Beth blushed bright red right down to her golden-brown roots. She had made love with a man she had known for little more than a week, not once, but three times. What in the world had she been thinking of?

She hadn't been thinking at all, she reminded herself. That was the problem. For the first time in her life, she had allowed her emotions to rule her actions. And God forgive her, but she wouldn't change a moment of it, even if she could.

She must be a little crazy, Mary Beth reasoned. Any second now she was bound to wake up and discover that it was all a dream. Or a nightmare. Either way, dream or nightmare, she was crazy about Nick Durand. And *that* was the truth.

From the beginning she had promised herself one thing. She would have no regrets. She was an adult. She had gone into it with her eyes open. She just hadn't expected to come out of it half-crazy in love with the man. No, it wasn't love. It couldn't be love. It must be infatuation. Sexual attraction. Nothing more. But it was enough. Oh yes, it was enough!

What did the future hold for Nick and herself? She didn't know and she didn't want to think about it. She was afraid to think beyond this day and this night. So she wouldn't. She wouldn't think about it. At least not now.

Mary Beth shook her head and came back to the present as Jacki was paying off the winners of that hand. Mary Beth won the hand and lost the next one. She had just ordered a ginger ale from the cocktail waitress when a young man staggered up to the table and threw himself down into one of the two empty seats beside her. Even with one empty stool between them, Mary Beth could smell the alcohol on his breath. And she could see the telltale glassy stare in his eyes. A rather pretty young woman came up and stood behind him. They were both dressed in faded denims and they both needed a haircut.

The young man plunked a bottle of beer down on the green felt table and dug around in his back pocket until he came up with a worn leather wallet. His hands were shaking. He couldn't seem to make them stop. The girl's fingers dug into the shoulders of his denim jacket, but not before Mary Beth saw her nails. They were chewed down to the quick.

There was something about the pair that immediately bothered her. Mary Beth told herself that it wasn't the way they were dressed. It wasn't their long, shaggy hair, or even the girl's pathetic fingernails. She liked to think that she had learned long ago not to judge a book by its cover. She was more of a humanitarian than that.

No, it wasn't the couple's appearance that bothered her as much as an air that clung to them when they walked up to the table. It was a feeling, a feeling of desperation that they brought with them. That's what was really bothering Mary Beth. They were desperate, and it showed.

She watched as the young man took a handful of crumpled bills from his wallet and threw them down on the table. Three hundred dollars on a single hand! Mary Beth closed her eyes for a moment and felt the air catch in her lungs. Surely he couldn't afford to be betting that kind of money.

All around the table, one after the other, the players fell silent. The easygoing camaraderie they'd enjoyed only moments before had vanished.

The hand was played out in deadly silence. A general sigh of relief went up from everyone at the table when the young man won. Mary Beth wasn't the only one who was hoping and praying that the couple would take their six hundred dollars and leave now while the going was good.

But it wasn't to be. The young man grew cocky. He took a long swig of his beer and carelessly tossed four bills onto the table. Mary Beth felt her heart settle somewhere in the region of her stomach. But it wasn't the young man she felt sorry for, it was the girl standing behind him. It was the girl with her unkempt hair and her dark, desperate eyes who reached out and touched Mary Beth's heart. She couldn't be much more than twenty or twenty-one. Barely old enough even to be legally permitted inside the casino.

Dear Lord, the things a woman would do for the man she loved, whether he deserved that love or not. This pathetic young woman was standing by her man even though it appeared he was foolishly, desperately, gambling all of their money on the luck of the cards.

Mary Beth's hands were suddenly freezing cold. Any fun she might have been having was gone. Long gone. It was as though the glitter and the glamour and the fantasy of Las Vegas itself were somehow being stripped away right before her eyes. It wasn't fun anymore. It was awful. It was ugly, she realized, trying to swallow the sour taste in her mouth.

The young man lost the next hand, and even the dealer seemed uncomfortable as she took the four one-hundred-dollar bills and stuffed them into the drop box at her elbow.

"Sir, are you sure you want to keep playing?" Jacki inquired before she dealt out the cards again.

She was answered with a dark, disdainful scowl as the young man took out his last two hundred dollars and slapped them down on the table.

It was the last straw for Mary Beth Williams. Something shattered inside her, breaking into a thousand irretrievably tiny pieces that could never be put back together again. She blinked back the scalding hot tears that sprang to her eyes. Scooping up her chips from the table in front of her, she dropped them into her evening bag.

"I—I'm sorry, everyone," she stammered, stumbling to her feet. "I can't just sit here and watch this.

It—it isn't fun anymore. And, dammit, it's supposed to be fun!'' she cried out, accusing no one in particular. "This—this is pathetic. It's heartbreaking!'' Her voice broke on the last word. She paused for a moment, wiping at her eyes, trying to collect herself. Then she reached out and touched the girl's arm consolingly. "I'm sorry. I am truly sorry.'' Then she turned her back on the young couple and forced her way through the crowd.

There was only one thought on Mary Beth's mind. One name on her lips. Nick Durand. What had Nick told her he was going to do while she played blackjack? That's right, he was going to check out a poker game. But where were the damned poker tables?

Mary Beth wandered through the casino, half-blinded by the tears swimming in her eyes. It was all coming down around her. The rose-colored glasses had been torn mercilessly from her eyes and all she could see now was the ugliness. The ugliness and the gaudy, garish colors and the loud, cheap music. She suddenly wanted nothing more than to get out of here and as far away as possible. She had to get away!

Oh God, where was Nick?

Nick Durand glanced down at the cards in his hand, then tossed a stack of chips onto the pile growing in the center of the table. "I'll raise you ten dollars,'' he said to the man sitting across from him.

The man stared back at him. He didn't know quite why, but he didn't think the tall, dark stranger was bluffing. Men like that didn't bluff. They didn't need to. But, dammit, he was holding a king-high straight with one card yet to go, and he didn't bluff either. "I'll call your ten and raise you another ten dollars."

Nick nodded and threw in ten more, then he casually glanced up from the poker game.

For an instant, his heart stopped beating.

Mary Beth was coming toward him, tears brimming in her soft brown eyes, tears threatening to stream down her face at any moment. Her hair was a little mussed and there was a wild look about her that he didn't like. He didn't like it one bit. She looked beautiful, but she looked like hell, as if she was going to burst into tears or get very sick. She came closer, and he could make out his name on her lips.

He didn't think twice. He didn't think about the hundred bucks he had in the middle of the table or about the full house he was holding in his hand—a full house that would surely win him the entire pot.

"I'm out," Nick said abruptly, throwing in his cards. Grabbing his remaining money from the table, he got to his feet. There was a stunned silence around the poker table. He wasn't the only one who'd expected him to win the sizable pot.

"Nick!" He clearly heard the raw emotion and something akin to pain in Mary Beth's voice.

Quickly he was there with his arms around her, shielding her from a dozen pairs of curious eyes. "My God, what's wrong, honey? Are you all right?"

Mary Beth squeezed her eyes shut. She hated making a fool of herself like this in front of people. "Yes, I'm all right." She swallowed the hot, salty tears that ran down the back of her throat. "No, I'm not all right,'' she whispered forlornly. She wouldn't have fooled Nick for long anyway.

There was a controlled savagery in the man's voice when he demanded to know, ''Are you hurt? Are you sick?''

The breath shuddered in her lungs, her stomach lurched precariously. ''No, I don't think so.''

With his arm around her shoulders, Nick took command of the situation. ''C'mon, let's get the hell out of here. You can tell me all about it once we're outside.''

He steered her through the crowd toward the door to the casino, but not before Mary Beth turned and looked back over her shoulder at the blackjack table she'd left five minutes before. The young man was still there, he must be winning at least some of the time, and the girl was with him. But Ralph and Margaret and the others must have followed her lead and left soon after she did. All of the seats at the table were empty except for one.

Mary Beth shook her head sadly. Her tears were wasted on a young man like that. But then she'd known that from the moment he sat down. Her tears were for the utter futility of it all, for the great sadness she'd seen in the girl's eyes, for so very many things she wasn't even capable of putting into words.

Or had her tears simply been for herself all along?

Nick was being very gentle with her, but she didn't know if she would be able to find the words to explain to him what had happened to her back there. She wasn't certain she understood it herself. All she knew was something had changed, drastically. Nothing looked the same to her. Nothing *was* the same.

"Do you want to walk for a while?" he inquired once they were outside the casino in the warm summer night.

"Yes, please, let's walk," she said through numb lips.

And they did. They walked for an hour, perhaps two. For the first time since her arrival in Las Vegas, Mary Beth Williams began to see things clearly. She saw them, not as she wanted them to be, not as she *wished* them to be, but as they were. That was the reality of living, she sighed. The rose-colored glasses had been removed from her eyes forever. It was time she planted both of her feet back on old terra firma. It was time she took a good hard look at what she had done, at whom she had tried to become.

There was no sense in denying that she was attracted to Nick Durand, terribly attracted to him. She would never have slept with him if she hadn't been. But there had been no mention of love or commitment by either of them. And what kind of future could she have with the man, anyway? He lived in a small town in Nevada, and she halfway across the country.

No, it would be best to think of this past week with Nick as a shipboard romance, as a few moments of stolen splendor. It was the only way, the only way. She would have no regrets, Mary Beth told herself sternly. She *must not* have any regrets. There was no future in it.

"Do you want to talk about what happened now?" Nick prompted as they came back around the corner by the Golden Nugget.

Although she would have preferred a less intimate setting, they could scarcely talk in public either. "Yes, I want to talk about it now, but not here, Nick," she said, looking around the busy, bustling hotel. "Let's go up to my room." They were in the elevator before she thought to ask him, "Did you lose much money by leaving the poker game like that?"

His hesitation in answering her was almost imperceptible. "Not much."

Mary Beth didn't believe him. "I'm sorry, Nick," she started to apologize profusely. "I know you left the game on my account. I'll be glad to reimburse you for whatever you lost." The minute the words were out of her mouth, she wished them back. But it was too late. Too late.

The man's whole body stiffened and his eyes narrowed into two chips of hard, black coal. "Dammit, Mary Beth, the money doesn't matter!" he grated, his voice cold and clear.

She'd only made matters worse and she knew it. How was she ever going to make him understand what had happened at that blackjack table tonight when she wasn't sure she understood herself? She unlocked the door of her hotel room and flipped on the light switch.

"Brrr, it's cold in here," she commented, heading for the air-conditioning unit. "I must have left the thermostat on low when we went out this afternoon." She turned the dial up, then swung around to face Nick.

The bed was between them. The bed where they had made love together that morning. It seemed like a lifetime ago. Mary Beth moved self-consciously to the other side of the room.

"Now would you like to tell me what the hell's going on?" he growled, his impatience beginning to show.

Mary Beth paced back and forth across the room. She inhaled deeply and began. "This may sound silly to you, Nick." Damn! That wasn't the way she'd intended to start. She took another deep breath and tried again. "I was sitting at a dollar blackjack table with a very nice group of people tonight. We were talking and playing cards and having a good time. No one was winning much, but no one was losing much either." She looked down at her hands and realized they were clasped together so tightly that her knuckles were white.

Nick stood there, staring at her broodingly. "Go on."

She dropped her hands to her sides and forced herself to continue. "A young man came up and sat down at our table. It was pretty apparent that he'd been drinking heavily. There was a girl with him. From the looks of it, they didn't have much money. Anyway, the kid took out this old wallet and plunked down three hundred dollars on the table. I couldn't believe it, Nick. I don't think anyone could. You should have seen the look on the girl's face." Mary Beth tried to swallow the tears that suddenly threatened to choke her.

"Why don't you sit down, honey?" Nick suggested, softening, gesturing toward the red velvet settee behind her.

"I think I'd prefer to stand right now, thank you," she murmured, shaking her head agitatedly. "Anyway, the young man lucked out on the first hand and won. I know everyone at the table was hoping he'd take the money and leave then, but he turned around and bet four hundred dollars on the next hand and lost! That's when I realized that I was furious." Her eyes were ablaze even now, glistening with unshed tears. "I was furious at him for ruining our fun—mine and all of those other innocent people at the table. But I felt so sorry for that young woman. I wanted to help, but I felt so helpless." She wiped her cheek with the back of her hand. It came away wet. "I—I didn't know what to do, Nick."

He took a step toward her. "Oh, sweetheart—"

She didn't hear him. "And do you know what that crazy fool did next? He bet his last two hundred dollars on another deal of the cards. I couldn't stand to watch for one more minute! I jumped to my feet and walked away. All I could think about was getting as far away from that place as possible, from this place, from Las Vegas!" Her voice rose on a crescendo of emotion. "I had to find you, Nick. I had to tell you. I want to go home. I want to go home to Wisconsin!" Mary Beth clamped a hand over her mouth. She hadn't meant to say that. But now that it was out in the open, she realized it was true. She *did* want to go home.

The man simply stared at her for a minute, his mouth set in a disbelieving line. "You want to go home because some fool kid, some stranger, got in over his head at the blackjack table?"

"Yes! No! Oh don't you see?" Mary Beth cried out, beseeching him to see, the tears streaming down her face now. "It's so much more than that. Don't you see, Nick? It's all of this." Her arms seem to encompass the man, the room, the whole town. "None of this is real. There's nothing behind the bright neon lights and the ringing bells and all the fun. That's the truth about this fantasy—it isn't real. There's nothing to it."

Nick's handsome face darkened like gathering storm clouds in a desert sky. "Let me get this straight, sweetheart." He twisted the word as he spoke it, lacing it with undisguised sarcasm. "You want me to believe that you saw a young man gambling away what may or may not have been the last of his money, and on the basis of that you want to pack your bags and head for home?"

"Oh God, I was afraid you wouldn't understand," groaned Mary Beth, her hands splayed across her abdomen as if she were somehow holding herself together by the sheer force of her will and nothing more. Her emotions were raw, exposed, like an open wound, and she was hurting. Dear God, he must see how much she was hurting! "How can I make you understand?"

Nick shook his head. "I don't know that you can. It looks to me like you've gotten yourself worked up into some kind of semihysterical state for nothing. I mean there are winners and there are losers everywhere, not just here in Las Vegas. It happens every day in the courtroom. That's life, sweetheart. And I'm afraid there is no magic cure for living," he told her in one of those superior tones of voice that men sometimes use with hysterical women.

"Don't patronize me, Nick Durand!" Mary Beth ground through her teeth. She was furious with him for being a man, and she was furious with herself for giving in to something as traditionally female as tears. "I was afraid you wouldn't understand. I should have known you wouldn't." It was a blatant accusation. It said he had all the sensitivity of a toad. It said that he was no different in the end than Jeffrey or her father. He was just another pretty face! Another perfect example of a man with more form than substance!

"And do you know what I think?" Nick came back in his own defense, taking a menacing step toward her. "I think this sudden attack of hysterics is about something else altogether. I don't think it has anything to do with that damned fool kid at the blackjack table."

Mary Beth shrank back from him. The man's physical presence was overwhelming, and a little frightening, no matter how much she argued with herself to the contrary.

She did manage to put her chin in the air. "What else could it be?"

Nick laughed, and it wasn't a very nice laugh. "You. Me. Us. Last night. This morning in *that* bed. And in *that* order." It was there between them like some kind of no-man's-land. "I don't think you can face the fact that we went to bed together, lady. Well, we did, and it's a little late to be having second thoughts." His handsome features tightened. "Why don't you try being honest with yourself for once? What's really bothering you is the gamble you took right here in this room."

Mary Beth tried to tell herself it wasn't the words themselves that hurt; it was the way Nick said them. But her chin and lower lip trembled in spite of her efforts to firm them with her teeth. "I told you in the beginning that I wasn't much of a gambler."

"Well, you can't just walk out and pretend it didn't happen," he smirked knowingly. "We're not two strangers anymore, Mary Beth Williams. We made love together. We're lovers."

"No! No, what we are, Nick, what we *were*, is a one-night stand. Love had nothing to do with it. What we had was sex, pure and simple."

"Like hell it was, lady librarian. You don't know the first thing about either one: sex or love. What we had together last night *and* again during the night *and* this morning was a whole lot more than just sex. We made love, lady." Nick's eyes showed a stubborn and still angry light, but his deep voice was growing softer and softer with each word as he moved closer and closer to her. "We're damned lucky to have found each other, Mary Beth. Surely you can't believe that what we have together is something that comes along every day." He was close enough to touch her now, and he did, one hand caressing her arm, one fingertip creating chills up and down the length of her spine. She could sense the anger still in him, under control, barely leashed, but no longer directed at her. "We're right for each other, honey. I know it. I feel it. You must feel it too.''

Masculine charm was one temptation Mary Beth Williams had had no trouble resisting in the past. Well, practically no trouble. But she'd never tried to turn her back on a man who attracted her as much as Nick Durand did.

"I—I don't think we are right for each other. I don't think you're right for me. You''—she swallowed hard—''you excite me, yes.'' Under the circumstances how could she deny it? ''But you overwhelm me, Nick. You frighten me. In fact, sometimes you scare the living hell out of me. I don't think fear is a good foundation to build a love affair on.'' She could feel him watching her with those nearly black eyes of his as she rambled on, weaving a web with her own words, only to be caught up in the web herself. ''I'm not the right woman for you, Nick.'' She smiled tremulously, sadly. ''I'm not the kind of woman who's cut out for a love affair, anyway. I'm far too conventional. Too old-fashioned. Call it anything you will. It all comes down to one thing. I'm not the woman for you.''

Nick put both hands on her shoulders. ''Has anyone ever told you that you think too much? For once in your life, Mary Beth, just *feel*. You know how good we feel together. How well we fit together. How much we belong together.'' He gave her a little shake. ''Trust your instincts. How can you believe we aren't right for each other when we're so damned good together?''

She pulled back, her voice sharp with tension. ''No!''

His fingers dug into her flesh right through the material of her kerchief and sundress. "Yes! We're right for each other. I know it. Dammit, honey, I know it!"

Mary Beth recoiled from him, and nearly shouted, "We're not! We're wrong for each other!"

Nick seemed stunned. "Do you really believe that? You can't believe that. We're fundamentally the same kind of people, honey. We're not afraid to dream. We're not afraid to go after what we want. We're not afraid to love."

Her voice was no more than a strangled whisper. "I am, Nick. I'm afraid."

He couldn't accept that. "You aren't! You aren't afraid to dream. What about Australia and the Great Barrier Reef? What about standing at Stonehenge at dawn to watch the sun come up?"

"There's a barricade around the place," she told him with bitter emphasis, her voice growing as hard as the shell she seemed determined to build around herself. "You can't even get close to the megaliths. Vandals, you know." She shrugged and pulled away from his hands, needing to put some distance between them. "But that's life. That's reality, Nick, as you seem so fond of reminding me. I know you think I'm a coward. Maybe I am. Maybe I'm not as brave as either of us thought."

Nick's eyes filled with promise. "You can be. Let me help you to be brave."

Cool shadows enveloped her. "You can't help me to be brave. No one can help me. No one can make me into something I'm not. Don't you see?" Her voice was husky with weariness. "We're not real. None of this is real. Not here. Not in this time and in this place.''

''What the hell are you talking about?'' he demanded a little savagely.

Mary Beth turned her head and stared searchingly at him. ''I told you last night, Nick. You are the man of my dreams, the man of my fantasies.''

Along with comprehension, came a look of cold, dark fury on his face. ''Are you trying to tell me that you used me to live out some erotic fantasy you'd dreamed up?''

''I wouldn't have put it quite like that,'' she said, after the briefest of pauses.

''Then how would you have put it? And what the hell are you, anyway? Some modern day member of the Miss Lonelyhearts club?'' The man's eyes narrowed into two black slits. ''What am I to you, Mary Beth? A trophy, a souvenir you wanted to take home from your Las Vegas vacation?''

She closed her eyes against what she saw in his. ''Please, Nick, don't!''

''Please don't *what*? Please don't tell you the ugly truth?''

''No,'' she said miserably.

''Well, if not that, then what?'' he demanded. He stood there, studying her for a minute or two, his angry stance gradually giving way to watchfulness. ''I'll tell you one thing. You'll never convince me that you're not at least a little in love with me. Not after last night. Not after this morning.''

The words came hard to Mary Beth. ''A woman can enjoy sex without emotional commitment.''

Nick was more than a little skeptical and it showed. "There are women who undoubtedly can, but you're not one of them, sweetheart. It's not your style and we both know it."

Mary Beth began, then swallowed roughly. "And what would you know about my style?" She untied the kerchief from around her shoulders and tossed it casually on the bed. "All right, if you must know, it was very good last night. You lived up to each and every one of my fantasies. But the fun's over, Nick. It's time we both got back to the real world." She looked up at him meaningfully. "But don't think that I haven't enjoyed this week—because I have." From the thankful tone she managed to instill in her voice, she might as well have slipped him a tip for a job well done and sent him on his way with a pat on the rear.

He put his head back and laughed. It was a sound of astonishment. "I can't believe this!" Nick planted both hands on his hips and stared at her, incredulity written on his face. The muscles of his arms flexed involuntarily by the action, his formfitting jeans emphasized the strength of his thighs, the long length to his legs. He had never looked so good to her, or so threatening. He laughed again, but Mary Beth could tell he wasn't really amused. "And here I thought you were only bright and intelligent, sensual and sweet—if a little emotional at times. I never figured you for stupid, Mary Beth."

She felt the hair stand straight up on the back of her neck. "And you, Nick Durand, are nothing but a slick, two-bit cowboy! You with your fine suits and your expensive gold watch and your handmade leather boots. Well, maybe you'd better look again. Maybe there's still a little cow dung stuck on the heels of those fancy boots of yours. And I don't give *that* for your opinion, mister!" She snapped her fingers together. "In fact, you can take your lousy opinions and go straight to hell for all I care!"

That quickly the man was across the room and had her by the arm. "If that's where I'm going, then that's where you're going too, sweetheart!" Nick promised with a fierce growl, looking as though he couldn't make up his mind whether to kiss her or strangle her. Perhaps it was all the same to him in the heat of the moment. Then he bit off a brief, but explicit, obscenity and released her arm. "God, woman, you could end up driving me crazy!"

"Then perhaps you'd better leave before I do," she pointed out to him with infuriating logic.

"You're damned right I'm leaving! There's obviously no sense in staying here for one more minute." Nick turned on his heel and reached the door of the hotel room in three angry strides. With his fist wrapped around the doorknob, he paused and looked back over his shoulder at her. "I'll talk to you in the morning, Mary Beth Williams. Once you've had a chance to calm down and come to your senses." Then he was gone, the door closing behind him with an uncompromising bang.

It was a full thirty seconds before Mary Beth could even think to react. "Once *I've* had a chance to calm down and come to *my* senses!" she sputtered furiously, her hands clutched in fists of frustration. Of all the insensitive, egotistical, incredible...the absolute nerve of the man!

Then she put her face in her hands and burst into tears.

Mary Beth Williams cried more that night than she had thought humanly possible. Then she dried her tears, bathed her face in cool water and calmly, methodically packed her bags. Then she called the airport.

She checked out of the Golden Nugget Hotel at the crack of dawn and took a taxi cab to McCarran Airport. There, she caught the "early bird" flight to Chicago.

It was somewhere over the majestic Grand Canyon, or the great patchwork quilt of the midwestern farmlands, that her own words came back to haunt her. It was something she remembered from that day at the country club with Julie. Surely, a day that was a thousand or two years ago.

It was the day she had arrogantly claimed she had nothing to lose by coming on this trip to Las Vegas. It was the day she'd decided that it was high time she learned to live a little. It was the day the old cliché paraphrased itself in her head. What was it? *Unlucky at love, lucky at cards.* Yes, that was it.

It seemed that in the end, Mary Beth had indeed gambled and lost.

Seven

Ah c'mon, Mary Beth, say you'll come with us to-night. What have you got to lose?'' Julie pointed out as she took two cups and saucers from the cupboard above her head.

She set them on the kitchen table and turned back toward the stove. The teakettle on the front burner was whistling for all it was worth. Julie quickly picked it up and poured the boiling water into the ceramic tea-pot on the counter. Then she carefully set the hot ket-tle to one side, slipped a quilted cozy over the teapot and carried it to the table. She set it down between them and then sat down again herself. It would take a few minutes for the tea to brew properly.

Julie Metzger always enjoyed drinking tea in the kitchen of the Williamses' house, although she pre-ferred coffee anywhere else. Somehow this large, light, airy room, overlooking a rather formal garden, went together with a cup of tea. It was no different today, she thought, gazing out the kitchen window at a perfectly symmetrical bed of red and pink geraniums, big bursts of white chrysanthemums all in a row and at least a dozen bushes of carefully pruned American Beauty roses.

Julie frowned and turned back to the disconsolate young woman sitting across the table from her. "What do you say, Mary Beth? Why don't you come to the dance with us?" she urged.

"I don't know, Julie," her friend murmured unenthusiastically.

She tried a slightly different ploy. "There'll be lots of singles there tonight. No one will even notice if you're alone."

Mary Beth shrugged her shoulders; it was a halfhearted gesture at best. "I know you mean well, but I really don't feel like going out."

Biding her time, Julie Metzger busied herself with pouring their tea. She waited until Mary Beth had added milk and sugar to her cup before she said what was really on her mind. "Look, Mary Beth, we've been friends for a long time, most of our lives, in fact. And I've always been aware that there was a very definite line drawn that I wasn't supposed to cross with you. You keep your private thoughts private and I've tried to respect that over the years."

Mary Beth looked up from her cup of tea. She seemed surprised, and a little uncomfortable at the unexpected turn in their conversation. "Yes, I suppose you're right about that, Julie."

The statuesque brunette reached across the kitchen table and placed her hand consolingly on her friend's. "There's something wrong, isn't there? There's been something wrong since you got back from Las Vegas." Julie gave Mary Beth's hand a pat and sat back in her chair. "I know you find intimacy painful. I've known it since your mom got sick and passed away. I saw how much it hurt you, bewildered you when your father didn't behave like the loving, grieving husband you expected him to be. I watched your reaction to the young women he'd parade home in front of you. I could see how much it hurt you, and yet you never once talked about it."

"I couldn't talk about it," Mary Beth confessed, stirring her tea for no reason at all.

"I know," Julie said in a husky alto. "And I was there when you lost your grandmother and even then I saw you pick yourself up by the bootstraps and go on. You had as much guts as I'd ever seen in a woman." Julie pushed the mop of dark hair off her face and took a deep breath. She was just getting to the hard part and she knew it even if Mary Beth didn't. "But I've never seen you the way you've been for the past month. I've never seen you down and out. I've never seen you without hope. I never thought I would see you give up." Mary Beth opened her mouth, but Julie quickly went on before she had a chance to speak. "You came home from your vacation and spent the first week in bed. You haven't been yourself since."

"I wasn't feeling well, Julie, you know that," Mary Beth said in her own defense.

"I know. Las Vegas throat, that's what the doctor called it. But I also know that it's taken a lot longer than he diagnosed for you to bounce back to your old self."

"I've just been a little tired, that's all," Mary Beth said evasively, looking away. "I haven't missed any work. And the days I was sick were still part of my second week of vacation."

Julie looked at her and said frankly, "I know. But whenever I stop by the library to go to lunch with you, or come by the house, you look like you're on your last legs, like it's all a little too much for you."

"I'm sorry. I didn't realize you were so concerned. I didn't mean for you to worry about me," she replied, her face clouding.

"Well, I have been worried about you, and if you don't tell me what's wrong or do something about whatever it is that's eating at you, you may very well drive us both crazy!" Julie blurted out.

Big tears welled in Mary Beth's eyes and her friend's mouth fell wide open. How long had it been since she'd seen her friend cry? Not in years. Not since they buried Abigail Williams on a fine spring day five years ago. A spring day that Abigail would have considered wasted on all this funeral fuss, according to a then teary-eyed, twenty-two-year-old Mary Beth.

"Can't you tell me what's wrong?" Julie pleaded. "Is it Jeffrey?"

Dear God in heaven, don't let it be Jeffrey. She couldn't bear it if Mary Beth had found out that she was in love with that jerk after all.

Mary Beth wiped the tears from her face and laughed raggedly. "Of course it's not Jeffrey!"

Julie sent up a silent prayer of thanks. But if not Jeffrey, than what . . . or who? Inspiration struck. "Is it someone you met in Las Vegas?"

Mary Beth's head came up with a jerk, and suddenly Julie knew. Of course, she'd met someone in Las Vegas! Why hadn't she guessed it was something like that? Then she answered her own question. Because it just wasn't the kind of thing that happened to Mary Beth Williams, that's why. Still, she should have known it was a man. All the signs pointed to it. Her friend was in love, truly in love at last!

Big brown eyes stared at Julie, bothered and more than a little bewildered. "How did you know?"

"Actually, I didn't. I've just never seen you act like this before." After a long silence she said, "I—I can listen if you want to talk about it."

It was as though once the floodgates were opened, there was no holding her back. First the tears flowed, then Mary Beth told about how they had met, and how they'd spent their time together.

"We stayed out all night. The sun was coming up as we walked back to our hotel. I didn't wake up until nearly five o'clock the next afternoon."

Julie was flabbergasted. "That was Saturday. That was supposed to have been your wedding day."

"Yes, and I'd forgotten all about it until later," Mary Beth admitted, her tone matter-of-fact.

Julie couldn't help herself. She let out a whoop of pure delight. "Now that's one little piece of information I would love to pass on to ole Jeffrey the Ladykiller. That'd bring him down a rung or two on the ladder." She shook her head, relishing the thought. "If he only knew. If he only knew."

"Jeffrey a ladykiller?" hooted Mary Beth. "Believe me, Julie, when it comes to women—or anything else for that matter—Jeffrey Donnell is a rank amateur."

So that was it. "And this Nick is a pro?"

"A pro with a capital P. All six feet and more of him, from the top of his beautiful black-haired head right down to his handtooled, leather cowboy boots."

"Then Nick is a . . ."

". . . lawyer." Mary Beth obliged her by filling in the blank. "He's half of the law firm of Durand and Durand. His younger brother, Matt, is the other half. Although the original partners were his father and grandfather." She smiled beatifically. "Nick says there are so many aunts and uncles and other relations in that part of Nevada that they like to think of it as Durand country."

Julie wanted to be certain she had her facts straight. "So, he's at least six feet tall, his name is Nick Durand and he's a lawyer from Nevada."

"Yes, and we had a wonderful week together, Julie. We went everywhere and we did everything. We took an Air Nevada tour to the Grand Canyon for a day. We went boating and picnicking at Lake Mead. We saw shows and we shopped and Nick taught me how to play roulette and baccarat and dice." Her brown eyes were huge and shining brightly. "The Friday night before I left, Nick took me to an exquisite French restaurant for dinner. It was one of those magical nights, Julie.'' She drew a breath and spoke slowly. ''It was the best night of my life—and I don't mean winning that jackpot I told you about.''

Julie smiled at her. ''I didn't think you did. So, you were with Nick Durand when you won the twenty-five hundred dollars.''

''Actually we won five thousand and split it down the middle.''

''I see.''

''That week in Las Vegas was the best week of my life,'' Mary Beth said wistfully, as though she were just realizing that fact for herself. ''I never wanted it to end.''

''But it did end, and you did come home. Almost a whole week earlier than you had originally planned,'' Julie felt obliged to point out.

Mary Beth sat up a little straighter in her chair. The wistful look on her face disappeared. It was replaced by something else, something that made her look— older. Older and wiser and experienced in a way that one woman always seems to recognize in another woman. It nearly broke Julie Metzger's heart to read what was written on that face. What had happened, for God's sake, to that dear, sweet innocence she had always adored in her friend? Who had managed to reach down deeply enough to tear at the very fabric of Mary Beth's heart?

All of a sudden, she wasn't sure that she cared one bit for Nick Durand. Not one damned bit!

Mary Beth sighed heavily. ''I never wanted it to end. But I knew then that I couldn't go on living in a fantasy world, in a world built on nothing more substantial than glitter and glamour. It was time for me to go home. It was time I started facing reality." She folded her hands in front of her on the table, but Julie could see they were trembling. "Nick didn't understand why I had to leave, of course, why I had to go home. He wanted me to stay. We quarreled about it, and he stormed out of my hotel room. He said he'd talk to me the next morning once I'd had a chance to calm down and come to my senses," she recounted heatedly.

Julie pointed her finger at her friend, and said accusingly, "You walked out on him, didn't you? You packed your bags and left Las Vegas without telling Nick." It was an inspired guess.

"Yes. Yes, I did."

"Why for heaven's sake?"

"Because...because I was afraid, Julie. I was afraid if I stayed I would wind up getting hurt." The words were wrung from Mary Beth like some deep, dark secret. She was about to confess aloud the very thing she'd tried to keep from admitting to herself for the past month. "I was afraid if I stayed I would end up so crazily in love with him that I'd make a complete and utter fool of myself over the man. So I walked before he had a chance to."

There! The truth was out at last. And they both knew it. For a minute or two, neither of them said a word.

Julie drew a sustaining breath and chose her words carefully. "There are worse things in this world, Mary Beth, than making a fool of yourself. Not that I've seen you even come close."

"Well, it's a moot point now," she sniffed, wiping her nose with a tissue. "It's all over. And I will get over him, Julie. I just need a little time. Someday I may even be a better woman for it. That's the kind of thing Abigail would have said." She turned her eyes away, knowing they would reveal her to be the awful liar she was. "Why, I can scarcely remember what the man looks like already," she said with such false optimism that Julie Metzger felt her own heart contracting painfully in her breast. "I think I will come to the country club dance tonight. I've been cooped up in this big old house long enough. It was time I got out and started having some fun again."

Julie heard the underlying desperation in Mary Beth's voice. There was a whole lot more to this story than she had been told. She was willing to bet on that. But the intimate details were none of her business. Some things were indeed meant to be kept private.

Still, it was a crying shame. A whole month had passed and there had been no sign of Nick Durand. She hated this feeling of helplessness, but what could she do? It looked as if her friend was going to learn this particular lesson about men the hard way. She could no more protect Mary Beth from that, than a mother could protect her children from growing up. That was life—painful though it might be at times.

"Well, I'm glad you've decided to go to the dance," Julie said affably, getting to her feet. She rinsed out her teacup and set it in the drain rack on the counter. "It's time I was going. I have a long list of errands to run today, and piles of dirty laundry waiting for me at home. By the way," she thought to add, "why don't you wear that luscious black taffeta you brought back from Las Vegas? That'll really wow 'em."

Mary Beth pushed her chair back and carried her teacup to the sink. "Wow *whom*?"

"Whomever," Julie laughed as she picked up her handbag and slipped the leather strap over her shoulder. "Some of the old gang and I will be by to pick you up around nine o'clock. There's Joe and his cousin Mitch from California, and I think Rob and Elaine may be going with us, too. Is that all right?"

"That's fine," Mary Beth said with a kind of polite indifference.

"Be sure to wear that black taffeta!" Julie called back over her shoulder as she scooted out the front door and down the sidewalk toward her car.

Mary Beth waved and closed the front door behind her. Then she turned around and leaned back against it. She squeezed her eyes tightly shut. "Damn!"

The solitary word echoed down the long hallway.

"Damn you, Nick Durand!" she cried out in a furious whisper, but she knew she was cursing herself as much as the man. Every last word she'd said to Julie was true until she had gotten to that part about scarcely remembering what Nick looked like. Then she had lied! Oh God, how she'd lied!

In truth, she remembered every detail of his face: the fine arch to his dark brows, the black, velvet depth to his eyes, the chiseled line of his jaw, the shape of his mouth. Lord, how could she ever forget that beautiful mouth of his!

And she remembered his body in intimate detail, as if it had somehow been imprinted on her mind and body for all time. How could she possibly forget the muscular breadth to his shoulders, the tapering leanness of his waist and hips, the strength in those legs and thighs? She wanted to forget, but she couldn't.

Mary Beth dragged herself back to the kitchen. She opened the refrigerator door and stood there, looking in at its meager contents. She should fix herself something to eat, but the thought of food nauseated her. She slammed the refrigerator door shut and poured herself another cup of the tea Julie had brewed earlier. It was lukewarm now and a light brown film formed along the rim of her teacup. She quickly dumped it in the sink and sat back down in her chair.

Perhaps it was time for some brutal truths. She not only remembered every detail about Nick Durand, but she'd longed for him every day and every night for the past month. She had longed for him until it left her feeling as if a terrible weight lay on her chest. No matter what she did, it was there, a constant reminder of what she'd left behind.

She hungered for Nick. She awoke in the middle of the night, an awful ache coursing through her, and she lay there stricken, knowing she had been dreaming of him, almost able to smell him, to taste him on her lips. She would lie there in the darkness and stare at the ceiling, knowing that he was walking quietly through the far recesses of her mind.

When had the man become so desperately vital to her? And how? How had he buried himself so deeply in her conscious and subconscious that there was no part of her heart or mind or soul that did not miss him utterly? Without him, the world was a different color.

Mary Beth stood in the big kitchen of her house and shivered. It was the middle of the summer and she was cold. Terribly cold.

Other women—thousands of women—had gone through the heartache of losing the man they loved. Somehow they had survived, she told herself. And she had survived losing so many of the people she had loved in her lifetime. She had survived this pain before and she would damn well survive it again.

Yes, first she would survive. She could always worry about *living* later.

Mary Beth automatically went through the motions of washing and drying the few dishes she and Julie had dirtied. What she needed now, she realized when that job was done, was good, hard physical labor. And plenty of it. She grabbed an old straw hat and gardening gloves that were kept in the mudroom between the kitchen and the back yard, and she headed straight for a large bed of pink petunias that needed weeding.

It wasn't the answer, but it would help.

"A Midsummer Night's Dream?" Mary Beth murmured as they walked into the ballroom of the Greensport Country Club at precisely nine-thirty that night. "It looks more like A Midsummer Night's Madness to me," she remarked to Julie and Elaine and the three young men accompanying them.

"Oh I don't know," laughed Julie, "I think I rather like it. Especially that incredible papier-mâché castle over there."

Now it was Mary Beth who was laughing delightedly. "That's not a castle, Julie. That's a tree." She looked around her with a kind of mordant curiosity. There were pasteboard cutouts of what were undoubtedly supposed to be Oberon, the king of Shakespeare's fairies, and Titania, his queen, and Puck and Wall and Lion and an unforgettable cast of extras, including a half-dozen or so smaller papier-mâché trees. There was pastel gauze everywhere.

Even the bandstand was draped in yards and yards of swirling, pastel gauze. The musical group playing for the dance tonight seemed right in their element in rhinestone-studded T-shirts, white tights and pink hair.

Julie Metzger shook her head. "I'd pinch myself if I thought it would do any good."

Mary Beth couldn't have agreed with her more. "I suddenly feel like I've been transported back through time and space to the ninth grade."

"Believe me, you never looked like *that* in the ninth grade, my dear, sweet Mary Beth," Joe teased, a big grin on his handsome face, his eyes sweeping her appreciatively from head to toe. "Now you two can stand here and admire the decorations all you want. The rest of us are going to find a table for six before they're all taken."

"We'll be along in a few minutes," Mary Beth replied, still blushing from the man's good-natured teasing. Good Lord, she'd known Joe Rankin since kindergarten. He was like a brother to her. And in all those years she could never once remember Joe flirting with her. Not once. The minute she was alone with

Julie, she glanced down at the strapless black taffeta gown. "Do you think it's too much?"

"Too much of what? Too much of you or too much of the black taffeta?" Julie remarked tongue in cheek.

"Julie!" Mary Beth dragged her friend's name through her teeth.

"All right, all right." Julie Metzger took a discreet step back and studied the dress for a moment. "No, it's not too much. Although I must confess I'm beginning to wonder just how much you have changed." She made a little gesture in the air with her hand. "I don't know, Mary Beth. Maybe it's the dress. Maybe it's the new hairstyle. I admit I thought we were going to see you with your hair pulled back in that ridiculous bun for the rest of our lives. And you are thinner. There's no doubt about that. Anything and everything you put on looks terribly chic on you." She shook her head, puzzled. "I don't know what it is, but you look fabulous."

That brought the color to Mary Beth's cheeks again. "Thank you, Julie. Between you and Joe, you're doing wonders for my battered ego. People do change, you know," she added at the last moment.

"They certainly do. Don't look now, but Jeffrey just walked in with Sheila Talbot on his arm."

"Sheila Talbot?" Mary Beth found herself choking on the blonde's name. "Why, she wouldn't give Jeffrey the time of day a couple of months ago."

"Oh, but have things changed since then!" Julie lowered her voice to a level of confidentiality. "When the whole thing blew up over your broken engagement and the Whitmans' broken marriage, Joanna

Whitman had to go home to her mother in disgrace. While Jeffrey, on the other hand, suddenly found himself with a reputation as a *rake*. A reputation that seemed to attract women like bees to honey. He's been going out with two or three different women this past month. Sheila Talbot's only one of them.''

Mary Beth just stood there, shaking her head and laughing to herself. And she had come back to *this* because it was supposed to be the real world! She felt more like Alice in Wonderland right here in Greensport than she ever had in Las Vegas. Nothing was as it seemed, not even here. There must be a very fine line, she decided, between fantasy and reality.

"Why, Mary Beth Williams, you look absolutely stunning tonight," came the familiar voice of a woman from behind her.

Mary Beth turned around and was surprised to see Josephine Weintraub standing there by the entrance to the ballroom. "Thank you, Miss Weintraub. You look very nice yourself," she said in response.

"I'm an official greeter for the dance tonight," the older woman explained as she looked about the room. "I can't take any credit for the decorations, of course."

Mary Beth could have sworn she heard the woman mutter "Thank God" under her breath, but she decided she must be mistaken. "How have you been, Miss Weintraub?"

"I couldn't be better, Mary Beth," she said cheerfully. When had Josephine Weintraub decided to start calling her by her first name? Didn't anything stay the same anymore? "I'm working for a bright young lawyer who's just located his offices here in town. Come to think of it, he's single. And I do believe he's here tonight. Would you like to meet him?''

Mary Beth was polite, but very firm in her refusal. "Thank you anyway, Miss Weintraub. But just lately I've had my fill of bright young men in general, and bright young lawyers in particular." She took hold of Julie's arm and turned her around. "You remember my friend, Julie Metzger, don't you?" She looked from one woman to the other. "Miss Weintraub has someone she'd like you to meet, Julie." Then she gave her friend a determined nudge. "I'll find the others and meet you back at our table later."

Julie looked back over her shoulder at Mary Beth, a slightly stunned expression on her face, as Josephine Weintraub took her by the arm and led her away.

Someday, Mary Beth thought, Julie would thank her.

Someday came much sooner than either of them expected. It was no more than fifteen or twenty minutes later that Julie Metzger showed up at their table with the handsome, young lawyer in tow. He was tall and blond and seemed totally captivated by the vivacious Julie. Julie, for her part, was all starry-eyed smiles.

Introductions were made all around, and a second table was pulled up next to the first one to make room for everyone. Then they settled down to having nothing more than a good time.

It was so much easier to keep up a brave front when she was in a group, Mary Beth was thinking to herself an hour later. If she didn't feel like talking all that much, no one seemed to take notice. And the music was loud enough that dancing was pretty much limited to just that—dancing.

"C'mon, Mary Beth, how about 'tripping the light fantastic' with me again?" Joe offered, holding out his hand to her.

She gave his hand an affectionate squeeze and shook her head. "Thanks anyway, Joe, but my feet would like me a whole lot better if I passed this trip."

"There's nothing wrong with my feet," Elaine hinted broadly as she came up to stand beside him. Like Mary Beth, she'd known Joe Rankin all of her life. And Elaine loved to dance, even if it was with a man who was like a brother to her.

Mary Beth popped a peanut into her mouth and turned her attention back to the animated conversation going on at the table. She was vaguely aware of someone sitting down in the empty chair next to her, but she didn't bother to look up until she heard an unwanted and all-too-familiar voice drawl, "You're looking good, Mary Beth."

She turned her head and discovered it was none other than Jeffrey Donnell beside her. Jeffrey looked very much as he had the last time she'd seen him. At least, that was Mary Beth's first impression. On closer scrutiny, she began to notice subtle differences. He was wearing his hair a little longer these days, although almost anything would have been longer than the near crew cut he'd sported in the past. His clothes were less conservative and his manner was most assuredly so.

He had a drink in his hand and she could smell the alcohol on his breath even at this distance.

How strange and how sad in a way that she had once imagined herself in love with this man. She felt nothing for him now. Not love. Not anger. Not even a desire for revenge. She felt nothing at all.

"Hello, Jeffrey," she said, deliberately instilling a kind of cool, aristocratic dignity into her voice.

"Hello yourself, and why so formal, sweetheart," he slurred, putting an arm around her shoulders. "By God, I think you're a little thinner. What's the matter? Have you been pining away for me?"

Mary Beth tried to shrug off his arm and failed. "They say a woman can never be too rich or too thin, Jeffrey," she informed him. Then she looked around the ballroom with seeming disinterest. "I heard you were here tonight with Sheila Talbot."

The man was confused. It was obvious that things weren't going as he'd planned. Assuming he had a plan in the first place, of course. "Yes, I'm here with Sheila tonight. She went to the powder room for a few minutes."

"And you took the opportunity to come over and say hello to me. Don't think for a minute that I don't appreciate the gesture, but shouldn't you be getting back to your table before Sheila returns? She might not understand, you know."

"I don't give a damn if Sheila Talbot understands or not," Jeffrey blurted out. "I want to dance with you, Mary Beth. You look so beautiful tonight. You never looked that beautiful when we were engaged."

He made it sound like some kind of accusation. "I want to dance with you, sweetheart."

Oh no, the man wasn't going to make a scene, was he? It was obvious he'd had too much to drink. And although no one else at the table even seemed aware of a potential problem, Mary Beth was growing uneasy.

"I'm giving my feet a well-deserved rest right now, Jeffrey. Thanks, anyway," she said, trying to dissuade him as politely as she could.

The man staggered to his feet and held out his hand. "I said I wanted to dance with you!"

Now they had the attention of everyone at the table. Out of the corner of her eye, Mary Beth could see the horrified expression on Julie's face.

"No thank you, Jeffrey!" she repeated a little louder and a little less diplomatically.

Before she could even guess what he was going to do, Jeffrey reached down and grabbed her by the arm, jerking her to her feet and none too gently.

"Dammit! Don't you start acting all high and mighty with me, Mary Beth Williams. And don't you go thinking you're too damned good now to dance with me!" he snarled nastily.

In the split second before it all happened, Mary Beth could have sworn she was being watched. It was the same unexplainable tingling sensation she'd felt that first night in the Golden Nugget before she had turned around to find Nick Durand watching her.

Her heartrate speeded up and her breathing started to come hard and fast. The hair on the back of her neck stood straight up on end and her body came strangely and wonderfully alive.

Then she heard Nick's voice cut through the noise of the crowd, and she stopped breathing altogether.

"Take your lousy hands off my woman, Donnell, or I'll break every bone in your body!"

Eight

Good Lord, it *was* Nick!

Mary Beth thought just for a moment that she might faint. She felt so light-headed. And her heart was slamming furiously against her chest. She swung around the best she could, considering that Jeffrey was still maintaining a firm grip on her arm, and stared up into those unmistakable black eyes.

Nick was no more than a foot or two from her. If she were to reach out, she could actually touch him. He was that close. He was standing there, dressed in one of those beautifully tailored suits of his, his hands resting on his lean hips, his feet braced slightly apart as if he were ready to spring into action at a moment's notice.

"I said, take your hands off her, Donnell!"

The command was repeated in a voice as cold and as threatening as any Mary Beth had ever heard. It left her quaking in her shoes.

"Who in the hell are you?" Jeffrey demanded belligerently, his once-handsome features screwed up into an unpleasant sneer. "And who the hell do you think you are to tell me to take my hands off Mary Beth or anyone else for that matter?"

Mary Beth thought she'd seen Nick angry. She was mistaken. She'd never see him like this. This must have been the tough streak of the early Durand men that ran in his veins. After all, they had been the kind of men who'd settled the Nevada territory practically singlehanded. There was something possessive, something violent in the way he stood there, glaring at Jeffrey Donnell.

She turned to the man holding her arm. "For your sake, Jeffrey, if not mine, let me go before he hurts you."

"Before he hurts me?" the man said laughing stupidly.

Mary Beth could see the tension and fear on every face around the table, men and women alike. It seemed everyone understood the true nature of the danger except Jeffrey. Jeffrey may have outweighed Nick by a good twenty pounds, but his wasn't the lethal, muscular weight of the older and taller man. One look at the two of them and only a complete fool wouldn't have known that Nick was the one to watch, that Nick was the dangerous one, the one you'd want on your side in a fight.

"He's been drinking, Nick," Mary Beth called out, either as a warning to him or as a partial excuse for Jeffrey's boorish behavior. She wasn't certain.

Something must have finally gotten through Jeffrey's otherwise thick skull. He suddenly let her go, almost hurling her toward Nick. "Hell, if you want her that bad, then you can have her. Believe me, she's not worth fighting over."

Nick caught her in his arms, staring down into her eyes for an instant as if reassuring himself that she was all right. Then he ordered, "Get behind me, Mary Beth, and stay there."

For once she didn't argue with him.

It seemed to happen all at once, then. Mary Beth stepping behind the safety of Nick's back. Jeffrey turning and taking a wild swing at him. Nick quickly and easily parrying the thrust. The next thing anyone knew, he had Jeffrey's arm pinned securely behind him, immobilizing him, removing the threat in a single, graceful movement.

"I'm not going to break your arm, Donnell," Nick growled as if he had to keep reminding himself *not* to do just that. "But if you every lay a hand on Mary Beth again, I'll break more, a whole lot more, than your damn arm. And that's a promise."

Then he shoved the man away from him with barely restrained violence. Mary Beth could feel the fury pouring from every pore of Nick's body. She'd never had a man ready to fight for her before. It was a new experience. A heady experience. A totally frightening experience she didn't think she'd care to repeat. Not in this lifetime anyway.

"Are you all right, honey?" Nick breathed through the tight clench of his teeth without taking his eyes off the other man.

"Yes. Yes, I'm all right, Nick," she murmured, reaching out to touch him at last—just her fingertips on the sleeve of his jacket. Even that sent a jolt through his body. She could feel it. It was the adrenaline still pumping through his veins. It wasn't something a man could turn on and off just like that. She understood now that there was a point of no return in both physical violence and sexual excitement.

Jeffrey stood there, rubbing his arm, silent and sullen and unhappily watchful. If he had any second thoughts about taking the stranger on—the stranger he noticed Mary Beth seemed to know well enough—they were permanently laid to rest by the look in the man's eyes. He'd never seen eyes so black or so cold.

Then he was distracted by the appearance of Sheila Talbot at his side. "C'mon, Jeff, dance with me," Sheila urged, her blue eyes big and wide with dismay. Apparently she'd been watching the entire incident.

"All right," he agreed, allowing her to take his arm and lead him to the other side of the dance floor, as far from the scene as possible.

It was conceivably the most decent act of Sheila Talbot's entire life, Mary Beth thought, as she watched the two of them walk away. Then she turned and looked up at the man standing at her side. She realized that her skin was strangely damp and her body all aquiver.

"Nick, what are you doing there?" she whispered uncomprehendingly.

"All in good time, Mary Beth. All in good time," he cautioned, taking a long, deep breath. "Right now I'd like you to introduce me to your friends. Then I'd like a drink. Then I want to dance with you. In that order."

With his arm securely around her shoulders, Mary Beth turned to the table of men and women, and introduced each one in turn until she came to Julie. "And this is the dear friend I told you about—"

"You must be Julie," Nick drawled, bestowing one of his utterly charming smiles on the brunette. "Mary Beth's best friend since the sixth grade."

"And you're Nick Durand." Julie had known it from the moment he walked in the door. With that purposeful stride and that beautiful black hair, it could be no one else. "Mary Beth has told me so much about you." But she was beginning to realize there were a few details Mary Beth had seen fit to leave out. Like Nick Durand was the most gorgeous male she'd ever seen. If he was half the man he seemed to be, then her friend was a lucky woman indeed.

Nick relaxed his stance, straightened his tie and smiled at her friends like the civilized human being he was—at least on occasion. "Sorry about the little disturbance, folks, but I don't like to see anyone manhandled. Especially a lady. Especially *my* lady. Now I'm sure you'll excuse us. I could use a drink."

As they walked away from the group around the table, Mary Beth could hear Joe Rankin exclaiming, "Jeez, did you see the way that guy moved! Donnell was a damn fool to take him on."

"Jeffrey has always been a fool." She recognized that sarcastic comment as coming from Julie. It occurred to Mary Beth that her best friend didn't like Jeffrey. In fact, she was beginning to suspect that she never had.

"By the way," Nick was telling her as they made their way toward the cash bar at one end of the ballroom, "there was a real nice woman out front who let me in once I explained to her why I had to see you. I think her name was—"

"Josephine Weintraub."

He blinked with surprise. "Yeah. How'd you know that?"

Mary Beth shrugged, and smiled up at him. "Would you believe a lucky guess?"

Nick tightened his arm around her waist as they sauntered up to the bar. "Do you want your usual?" She nodded. "The lady will have a frozen daiquiri. I'll have Scotch and water, please," he told the bartender.

With their drinks in hand, they managed to find a deserted corner behind one of the paper-mâché trees.

"What the hell are these decorations supposed to represent, anyway?" Nick growled impatiently as he pushed a tree limb out of his way.

"The theme of the dance is A Midsummer Night's Dream," Mary Beth explained before she put her head back and started to laugh. She laughed as she hadn't laughed in a month. It felt so good to laugh. It felt so good to be with Nick. Then she looked at the man and saw what was in his eyes, and it was no longer a laughing matter.

"God, how I've missed the sound of your voice!" he groaned as if it somehow caused him great pain to make that admission. Nick put his drink down and reached for her glass. "The hell with our drinks! I can't take this another minute. I have to hold you. I have to feel you in my arms. Dance with me. Dance with me, sweetheart."

He got to his feet and held his hand out to her and Mary Beth remembered another night when he'd held his hand out to her and she had gone into his arms as she was going into his arms now. Whatever else happened, there would always be this between them: this compulsion, this desperate need for each other, this physical attraction that neither could control or even begin to explain.

She went into Nick's arms and it seemed the most natural thing in the world. There was none of the initial awkwardness she had expected after one long month apart. Her hands slipped around his neck as he drew her body hard against his, and she melted.

Oh God, the man walked blithely back into her life after four long weeks and she was instantly putty in his hands! But she couldn't be! She mustn't be! There were so many questions. She had to know a few of the answers.

Mary Beth tried to put a little distance between them. "What are you doing here, Nick?"

"I'm here to see you, of course," he murmured, his mouth buried deeply in her hair. He seemed disinclined to elaborate.

"How did you get here?"

He put his head back and gazed down into her face. "That's not as easy as it might sound. Have you ever tried to make travel arrangements between a small town like Elko, Nevada, and an even smaller town like Greensport, Wisconsin?"

She shook her head. "No."

"Well, the first step was to charter a flight out of the Elko Municipal Airport to take me to Salt Lake City. There I made connections to O'Hare, and from there on to Madison. Once I hit Madison I rented a car and drove the last thirty miles to Greensport. I've been on the move since first thing this morning."

Mary Beth stared at him broodingly. He did look tired, but she had even more important things on her mind. "How did you know where to find me?"

"When I got to town, I checked into a motel long enough to shower and change my clothes. Then I got directions to your house. Nobody was home, but the guy down at the corner gas station seemed to think that almost everybody in town was out at the country club for a dance. So, I drove out here. Apparently just in the nick of time," he muttered, his arm tightening about her waist.

She pressed her face into the front of his jacket. The material was cool against her heated flesh. "I—I'm sorry about that scene with Jeffrey." She tried to swallow the awful lump in her throat. "I don't know what got into him tonight. I've never seen Jeffrey like that before."

A muscle in Nick's face started to twitch. He took one hand from her waist and tipped her chin until their eyes met. "Have you been seeing much of Donnell since you got back from Las Vegas?"

Mary Beth sucked in her breath. Surely, Nick didn't think that of her!

"No! No, of course I haven't," she denied vigorously. "In fact, this is the first time I've seen Jeffrey since we—since he broke off our engagement." A flicker of annoyance crossed her face as she stared off into space. "I can't imagine what I saw in the man in the first place."

"I can't either," Nick agreed, sounding suspiciously like a jealous lover.

"I haven't thanked you yet for coming to my rescue," she said, with a touch of anxiety.

"No thanks are necessary," he assured her.

Mary Beth's eyes narrowed. "You handled yourself like a pro back there."

"Hardly like a pro," Nick disagreed. "But where I come from, a man should know how to take care of himself and whatever is his. Donnell's a big man, but he's soft," he added brutally. "If he hadn't been so soft in the gut, I would have been tempted to lay my fist into him once or twice just to teach the bastard a lesson." It was a moment or two before Nick realized that the woman in his arms had suddenly gone very still on him. He bent down and dropped a kiss on her mouth. "Hey, darling, there's nothing to be frightened of now. I'm not going to hurt the guy as long as he stays away from you."

Mary Beth moved her mouth painfully, but it was some time before the words could be forced out between her lips. "When I was a young girl I used to love to read about the days of chivalry. King Arthur and his gallant men. The knights who would fight for a maiden's honor." Her eyes were huge now and very dark. "And I think every teenage girl dreams at one time or another about the two best-looking guys in school fighting over her." She looked up at Nick and there was an infinitely sad expression written across her face. "But the truth is, it's not gallant. It's awful. It's awful and it's frightening when two men resort to physical violence. It's not at all what I'd dreamed about."

Nick brought both of his hands up to gently frame her face. "My dear, sweet, innocent girl," he murmured huskily. "I wish I could be a white knight and stay up on that damned horse just for you. But I'm a man like any other man, Mary Beth. I make mistakes. I lose my temper. And not all the battles I fight are in the courtroom." Then he laughed lightly. "And here I thought you were such a pragmatist when I first met you. You, my dear woman, are a dreamer. A dreamer and a romantic."

"You make it sound like some kind of curse," she said defensively.

His eyes were like the summer night: all soft and dark around the edges. "No, not a curse, Mary Beth, but a blessing. It's a blessing to see life through the eyes of a romantic. Don't you know it's one of the things I adore about you most?"

"No, I didn't know," she whispered.

"Even the dress you're wearing is romantic," Nick said, his voice oddly hoarse. "I'll never forget that night I stepped off the elevator at the Golden Nugget and saw you standing there, all black taffeta ruffles and skin like ivory silk."

Then he bent his head and his lips skimmed her bare shoulder, and she shivered down the length of her spine. He seemed intent on inhaling the very essence of her skin, taking it in through his sense of smell and taste and touch.

"My God, Nick!" she breathed, forcing him to lift his head. She looked quickly around them. "Please, don't! Someone will see us."

"Then we'll go someplace where they won't," Nick promised, dancing with her toward the discreet corner where they had left their drinks.

The minute they were shielded from view, he backed her up against the wall of the ballroom, his hard body pressing into hers as his arm went around her.

"This is all I've thought about, all I've dreamed about for the past month!" Then his mouth swooped down and captured hers, and all around them the night went still.

He was hungry, urgent, desperate for her. And Mary Beth found her mouth opening to his with the same hunger, the same urgency, the same desperation. They couldn't get enough of each other. It would never be enough.

"Nick, no!" she cried out softly, dragging her mouth from his. "Not here!"

He cursed softly and took half a step back from her. His breathing was harsh, and it took a minute or two before he could speak. "We have to go someplace where we can be alone, sweetheart."

"Yes! Yes, but I want to tell Julie that we're leaving. It's the only polite thing to do since I came with her and the others," Mary Beth pointed out.

"And I'll go with you. I want to tell your friends what a pleasure it was meeting them. Then we'll politely say good night and get the hell out of here."

Mary Beth wiped the lipstick off his face and straightened his tie for him. Then she tried unsuccessfully to comb through her tangled hair with her fingers, and ended up giving it a good shake, hoping it appeared naturally windblown. They managed to wind their way back across the dance floor and make their farewells with a minimum of fuss.

"I'll talk to you tomorrow," Julie murmured as Mary Beth gathered up her evening bag and they were preparing to leave. "And good luck!" she called out after them.

"What the hell did she mean by that?" Nick wanted to know.

"I don't know for certain," brazened Mary Beth. "Perhaps she simply felt that I would need all the luck I can get considering the company I keep."

He had the good graces to appear at least a tad uncomfortable. "I guess I have a tendency to come on a little strong sometimes."

Sometimes! Mary Beth fought down the urge to laugh in the man's face. "I guess you could say that," she replied, making the understatement of the year.

"Ah, there you are, Mary Beth. Are you and your guest enjoying the dance?" Miss Weintraub inquired as they walked out of the ballroom and through the official entranceway of the country club.

"Yes, but I'm afraid we have to leave a little early tonight," Mary Beth said, without explaining. "I do want to thank you for allowing him in this evening."

"You're most welcome, my dear," Josephine Weintraub responded. "I see you found her, Mr. Durand."

Nick took the woman's hand in his—for a moment, Mary Beth wasn't certain if he was going to shake it or kiss it—and shook it firmly, but somehow intimately as well. "Thank you for your help this evening, Miss Weintraub."

She smiled back at the man, seemingly bedazzled by him. "Anytime, Mr. Durand. Anytime."

Mary Beth didn't say another word until they were safely out in the parking lot and on their way to Nick's rental car. "Do you have any future political ambitions?" she inquired, cocking her head to one side and looking up at him.

"I haven't really thought about it, but I don't think so." His tone conveyed a shrug. "Why do you ask?"

"Oh I was just wondering, that's all. You seem to have quite a way with the ladies, both young and old. Now the only question is, how good are you at kissing babies?"

"I don't know." Nick opened the car door and settled her in the passenger's seat. "Would you like to help me find out?"

"And how do you suggest I do that?" she inquired as he got behind the steering wheel and slid the key in the ignition.

There was the very devil in the man's eyes. "We could always go to your place and *make* a couple of babies for me to kiss."

Mary Beth felt the color rise to her face like cream to the top. "Do you always have sex on the brain?"

Nick Durand shook his handsome head and tried to appear innocent. It didn't work. "No. Although I have noticed that I think about sex a lot more since I met you."

"That's your problem, not mine," she sniffed, putting her aristocratic little nose just a little higher in the air.

"Oh, and I suppose in the past month you haven't once thought about us making love together?"

Mary Beth permitted herself a small sigh. "I didn't say that."

He merely smiled and crowed, "Then you have!"

"Well, yes, I suppose so," she admitted. He was confusing her, dammit!

"Well, yes, I would *hope* so!" Nick countered. "You're a perfectly healthy young woman with perfectly healthy sexual appetites. I can personally vouch for that." He pulled up at a stop sign and turned toward her. "And I'd hate to think that I was the only one who's lain awake night after night for the past four weeks. Seems more like four years to me," he admitted, every trace of humor gone now from his voice.

"Oh Nick—" That was all Mary Beth got out before her voice choked up. "Why is it I can never win an argument with you?" she asked some minutes later as he turned the car in the direction of her house.

"Sweetheart, I'm a lawyer. Winning arguments is my business," he informed her.

"Well, there's not going to be any argument about one thing, Nicholas James Durand. We are going back to my house and we are going to talk."

She could almost hear the snappy "Yes, ma'm!" that preceded his response.

"Whatever you say, Mary Beth," he meekly agreed.

Too meekly. She was immediately suspicious. "Now what are you up to?"

"Nothing. Absolutely nothing," Nick assured her. "If you don't believe me, you can look for yourself."

Mary Beth blushed. A hot, unmistakable blush right up to her ears. "You're enjoying every minute of this, aren't you?" she retorted accusingly.

"Of course," he admitted, smiling at her with that certain smile that always made her stomach do funny little somersaults. "Is there any reason why I shouldn't?"

Was there any reason why he shouldn't be enjoying himself at her expense? Damn right, Mary Beth swore to herself. The problem with their relationship was plain enough to her. Nick held all the cards. Even the deck was stacked in his favor.

It might work very nicely for a man to have an affair based on physical attraction alone, but it wouldn't work for her, Mary Beth acknowledged to herself. She'd go and fall in love with him, and in her mind that led to marriage and a home and children. She was old-fashioned. She was conservative. And she was proud of it.

Oh, Nick had talked about finding the right woman to spend his life with. He'd talked about marriage and a home and children, certainly, but never with her in mind. He'd never once mentioned any interest, any desire in marrying her!

She didn't say anything for a long while, but as he pulled up in front of her house, she simply sat there in the darkened car, her shoulders slumped in defeat.

"Aren't you going to invite me in?" he drawled in that sensuous way he had of speaking. She could hear the innuendo laced through every word he spoke.

"Look, Nick, I'm tired," she told him wearily. "Too tired to play any more clever word games or any more clever bedroom games with you. You're far too clever for me all around. So why don't you just drop me off here at my front door and we can discuss all of this another time?"

Then she opened the car door on her side and got out, digging in her evening bag for her house key as she walked toward the front door. The sound of a car door slamming behind her registered somewhere in her brain, but she didn't turn around and she didn't slow down.

She slipped the key in the lock and turned it, then pushed open the door of her house. She'd left a light on in the hallway. She didn't care to come home to a dark house. She dropped her evening bag on the hall table and finally turned around as she heard the front door close resoundingly behind her.

Nick was standing there. There was a look on his face she found impossible to read. He seemed angry, but not exceptionally so. He seemed determined, but about what she wasn't sure. He simply stood there for a moment: solid as stone and just as enduring, broad-shouldered and utterly beautiful. She could have wept.

Then she saw the duffel bag in his hand. It hit the floor and Nick kicked it aside.

"I didn't come halfway across the country to be told we'd discuss this another time, lady. I walked away from you once. I won't walk away from you again. Not unless you're ready to stand there and tell me you want to end it between us here and now." He flipped the lock on the door behind him. The small click echoed down the long hallway. Then the man took a step toward her. He was quiet and graceful and un-thinkably dangerous.

"Nick, please!"

"Go ahead, sweetheart. Tell me you don't want me. Tell me you don't love me. But don't expect me to make it easy for you!"

Nine

Damn you, Nick!" It was a far cry from anything original, but it expressed Mary Beth's feelings quite nicely.

Nick took another step toward her, the hard heels of his boots clicking sharply on the marble floor. He made an imposing figure, standing there in the front vestibule of her house, tall and broad-shouldered and larger than life.

The man's eyes burned like coals. "I already am damned to hell if you end it here and now, babe. I have nothing left to lose if I lose you," he said, planting his muscular legs in an uncompromising stance.

"I hate you!" The words were like a frantic curse she flung at him as she backed away.

"Sure you do."

"I don't hate you." She immediately took the words back.

"I know," he said, the hard line of his mouth beginning to soften at the edges.

She clasped her head between her hands and shook it distraughtly from side to side. "Oh God, why am I so emotional?"

"Maybe you're pregnant," Nick suggested thoughtfully as he took another step toward her.

That brought Mary Beth's head up with a jerk. "That's not funny!"

"I didn't say it to be funny," he told her, his intent gaze beginning to make her squirm a little uncomfortably.

"Well, I'm not pregnant. I can guarantee it," she shot back, taking several deep breaths in an attempt to calm herself.

He shrugged his shoulders. "I can't say that I think it's the perfect way for a couple to start out in a marriage, but if it had happened it wouldn't have made any difference in the long run. It's bound to happen sooner or later, anyway."

Mary Beth looked at him. "What's bound to happen sooner or later?"

He merely smiled and shrugged his shoulders again. "Your getting pregnant."

"What the hell are you talking about?" she snapped, placing her hands on her hips and glaring up at him.

Nick circled around her, his eyes studying her every step of the way. "You've gotten a little thinner since I last saw you, haven't you?"

"Perhaps I have lost a couple of pounds, but then it has been *four* weeks since you last saw me, Nick," she reminded him sarcastically.

He rubbed the back of his neck with one hand, while the other dove into the pocket of his perfectly tailored slacks. A familiar jingle could be heard as he absently toyed with the car keys and loose change. Then he sighed and looked at her with regret in his eyes. "And you'd like to know why it took me so long to come after you?"

She looked at him as if he was crazy. "No. I'd like to know why you bothered to come after me at all."

Nick started to say something, then changed his mind. Instead he held his hand out to her. "What do you say we call a temporary truce between us? It's been a long day, honey, and I never did get my drink back at the country club. Do you think you could spare something for a tired and thirsty man?"

"Yes, of course, I—I'm sorry," Mary Beth mumbled, knowing that Abigail Williams would no doubt turn over in her grave if she knew of her granddaughter's lack of hospitality. "Would you like a cup of coffee or tea, or something a little colder and stronger?"

"Actually, I would love a cup of coffee," Nick confessed, brushing his hand across his eyes.

There were a few tired lines around his eyes and mouth that she didn't remember seeing there before. What in the world had the man been doing with himself for the past month?

"If you'd like to take a seat in the living room, I'll go put the coffee on," Mary Beth said formally as she went around the front room, turning on a lamp here and there. She ushered him in with a wave of her hand, then left the room and headed straight for the kitchen. It took her a moment or two to realize that Nick was following right behind her.

"There's no sense in me sitting out there in the living room all by myself when I could be in here with you," he explained, shedding his coat and tie, and pulling up a chair. "I hope you don't mind."

"No, I don't mind," she said stiltedly, then busied herself with the preparations for making the coffee.

The silence grew between them for a moment. Then Nick cleared his throat and asked, "How have you been, Mary Beth?"

"All right," she said crisply, turning on the cold water and filling the coffeepot. They both knew her answer had told him nothing. "How have you been?"

"Busy. I've been involved in an important trial for the past month. We just wrapped it up yesterday," he said significantly.

"Did you win?" Mary Beth inquired as she took cups and saucers from the kitchen cupboard.

"Yes, we won."

"You don't take cream or sugar in your coffee, do you?"

"No, I don't." Then it seemed Nick had had enough, more than enough. His eyes suddenly went black. "I'll be damned if I'll sit here making small talk with you when what I really want to know is why you walked out on me in Las Vegas?"

So it was all going to come out in the end, Mary Beth sighed. She'd been expecting something like this since the moment Nick had stalked into the Greensport Country Club. He obviously hadn't traveled halfway across the country to go dancing with her. She would allow herself to remember. Perhaps it was the first step in learning to forget.

She poured their coffee and set the cups on the kitchen table, then sat down in the chair across from him. She folded her hands modestly in front of her. "Do you really want to go into all of this tonight, Nick?"

"The last time I waited until morning, I woke up to discover that you'd skipped town." His voice was bitingly sarcastic.

Mary Beth winced. "I guess I deserved that." She moistened her bottom lip. "What I tried to explain to you in Las Vegas was true, Nick. The fantasy was stripped away by what happened that night at the blackjack table. I can't tell you why it affected me so strongly. I only know that it did. After that, nothing seemed real. Nothing was the same. And that included you and me. Suddenly, it was tawdry and superficial. It was like the sparkle of gold that turns out to be fool's gold in the end."

Something of what she was trying to tell him got through this time. Or perhaps it was because he'd thought of little else for the past four weeks. Nick reached out and placed one of his hands over hers. "Just like it's hard to tell the difference between fool's gold and real gold, I guess it's hard to tell the difference between fantasy and reality sometimes."

Mary Beth paused reflectively. "I've been learning just how difficult it can be to separate the two since I got back home." She laughed mirthlessly. "Here I thought all along that Greensport was the real world and Las Vegas was only a fantasy world built out of bright lights and fancy hotels and shiny chromium slot machines." She threaded her fingers through his and stared at the strength of their entwined hands. "And it turns out the whole world's crazy, Nick. What difference does it make if it's a flashy casino in Nevada or a small-town country club decked out like some

fantastic version of a Shakespearean play, complete
with a pink-haired punk rock group? None of it's real.
None of it makes any sense.''

"Yes, the whole world's crazy, sweetheart, but it
can make sense. If two people love each other enough,
they can create their own little island of sanity amid all
the insanity," he said with conviction, his fingers
clasping hers tightly.

"But I was afraid, Nick, so afraid. That's why I
turned tail in Las Vegas and ran." Her throat choked
up with emotion. She was going to tell him everything
now. The man deserved that much. And she was going
to be strong enough to remember, so that one day she
could forget. "Don't you understand? I was falling
crazy in love with you, but I couldn't tell if it was real
or only a fantasy, only a dream." Her tears were like
shimmering drops of crystal poised on her eyelashes.
She impatiently wiped them away with the back of her
hand. "I was afraid I would make a fool of myself
over you, Nicholas Durand. I decided the only safe
way to deal with what I felt for you, was to convince
myself it was merely an infatuation. I would get over
you, if I went away and never saw you again."

"And did you get over me?"

"No," she confessed in a voice bruised with pain.

"Then that makes two of us, lady, because I didn't
get over you either," he said, his eyes dark with regret. "I told you in Las Vegas not to have any regrets.
But I've had plenty! When I think back to our last
night together and some of the things I said to you."
He bowed his head in self-disgust. "God knows how
sorry I am, Mary Beth. I called you silly and stupid,
and the truth is I'm the one who was stupid. I knew
how disturbed you were over the misfortune of that

young couple. You have a tender heart and I tramped
all over it like an insensitive son of a—''

"And I'm sorry I called you a two-bit cowboy."

His head came up, and there was that crooked little
smile on his handsome face. "With cow dung on my
boots, don't forget that part."

Mary Beth laughed, but there were tears in her eyes.
"I'm sorry about so many things, too, Nick."

"So am I, sweetheart. I was selfish. I rushed you
into a physical relationship I knew in my guts you
weren't ready for. But, dammit, our time together was
so limited! I needed you tied to me in a way neither of
us could ever dispute," he confessed staring into his
half-empty coffee cup. "Who am I trying to kid? I just
plain old wanted you. Everytime I got anywhere near
you, I wanted to kiss you, to touch you, to make love
to you."

"I felt the same way. I still do," she vowed, her
voice shaking with emotion.

Nick looked at her, his mouth twisted into a wry
smile. "There seems to be this compelling attraction
between us, you know."

She swallowed. "Yes, I know."

He paused, then expelled an expressive breath.
"What the hell are we going to do about it?"

Her eyes were huge. "I—I don't know."

Nick pushed his chair back and stood up. He came
around the corner of the kitchen table and took Mary
Beth gently by the arm, bringing her to her feet. Then
he firmly brought her face up to his. They were standing so close that his breath stirred the wisps of hair
around her face like a bittersweet summer breeze.

"There's something I've wanted to ask you for a
very long time, Mary Beth Williams." Nick's voice

didn't sound quite like him. "Do you know that I love you?" She couldn't even shake her head one way or the other. "Some men spend their whole lives loving the wrong woman. I know you're the right woman for me. But I'm going to love you, right or wrong, for the rest of my life."

It was sometime before she could even cry out softly, "But how can you be so sure that I'm the right woman for you? How can you know that we're right for each other?"

"Because life is a self-fulfilling prophecy. What we believe to be true, often comes true." The authority in his voice had its effect. "I am the right man for you, Mary Beth Williams. And you are the right woman for me. If we believe it to be true with all of our hearts and minds, then it will be true! You can say what ever you will, I believe that I'm the best damned thing that's ever happened to you. I know you're the best thing that's ever come into my life." His voice dropped to a whisper. "God, I can't imagine what my life would be like if I had to spend it without you. It scares me just to think about it." He stared down into her eyes, and once again she saw the desert night in their black velvet depths. "I guess it all comes down to one thing in the end, sweetheart. Do you believe in me, in the reality of our love, enough to marry me?"

"Yes." She went into Nick's arms then and it seemed the most natural thing in the world. She was coming home, truly coming home. There was none of the awkwardness she might have expected after a long separation. There was only a sense of homecoming.

She was gathered to him as if she was something very precious. His hands held her carefully as if he half-feared he might crush her. He wanted to hold her.

He wanted to touch her, yet he was afraid he might hurt her. They simply stood there, holding each other. Neither knew for how long.

Then Mary Beth said as calmly as she could, "I know now that there are worse things than being afraid to love. And that is to live a life without it. There's always a risk involved when you love someone. Love is a gamble. But it's worth the gamble, whatever the stakes," she murmured, her arms going around his waist. "You are all things to me, Nick Durand. You are the man of my dreams, the man of my fantasies, and the man of real flesh and blood in my life. You are real. And you're all I ever imagined a man could be. You are the best of both worlds. You're my fantasy and my reality. And I love you."

"And I love you, Mary Beth, with all my heart and my soul and my body," Nick pledged.

"We are right for each other," Mary Beth whispered. "I know that now. With you by my side, I won't fear this crazy world we live in. You give me the courage I need to believe in that island of sanity amid all the insanity of the world."

Nick held her to him fiercely. "I've always thought of myself as a man of words, but when I need them most they fail me. I wish there were words for me to say to you that no man has ever said to a woman. I wish there were sacred vows to repeat that no man or woman have ever sworn to each other. I'd like to believe that no man and woman have ever loved as we love. When I say that I love you, I want you to know that no man has ever meant it more."

Mary Beth brought her mouth to his. "And no woman has ever meant it more. I've missed you so, my love. And I've longed for you day and night."

"But not tonight," Nick vowed. "Tonight we'll be together."

Then they stepped apart only long enough to unplug the coffeepot, shut off the lights, and check the lock on the door before they climbed the stairs to Mary Beth's second-story bedroom.

They slowly undressed each other and stood there in the intimate surroundings of her bedroom, their skin bathed in the soft glow of a single lamp burning low on the beside table.

"You're even lovelier than I remembered," Nick said huskily as he laid her back on the bed.

Then he reached down and pressed his worshiping, adoring mouth to the inviting swell of her breasts, the firmness of her flat abdomen, the soft womanly mound that dipped between her legs. He left a trail of fire down her body. Her skin was sensitive to the slightest caress, the merest whisper of a kiss.

"Nick!" Mary Beth could scarcely breathe as her body responded breathlessly to his touch. She could feel her nipples tightening into hard, aching peaks that begged for his mouth. She arched her back instinctively and he caught her breast between his lips and suckled until she could feel the lovely, agonizing, aching need for him spread throughout her entire body.

For a moment, Nick let his weight press her into the mattress and she was literally, physically, overpowered by him. Her hands went to his shoulders, her fingers grasped the muscular flesh as her nails scraped sensuously along its surface. Her tongue wet her dry lips and then ventured forth to taste him: the smooth skin, the soft crinkle of man's hair, the thrill of hard, flexed muscle.

Then his mouth was on hers and she could taste the very essence of herself on his tongue. Mary Beth could feel and taste and smell him on her skin, just as surely as Nick must feel and taste and smell her on himself. It was a seductive, erotic, provocative thought. There was a kind of perfect symmetry, a natural beauty, to the way his body fit hers. The way their tongues met and moved in a sinuous dance. Her breast was made for his mouth, just as she was fashioned to take him, all of him, and rejoice in the taking.

Then he was there, coaxing, demanding, ready to have her take him into her body. She opened her legs and welcomed him, and he joined himself to her with an elemental, primordial need that was as much hers as his. He stroked her knowingly, igniting her with his kiss and with his touch.

His hand delved between them and he found that tiny, sensitive bud with his fingertip. A soft, feminine sound came from the back of Mary Beth's throat as he caressed her and at the same time thrust deeper into her body. The dual sensations filled her with a kind of wild thrill. She felt an overwhelming shudder take her in its grasp and hold her tightly until she nearly lost consciousness.

Then Nick anchored himself to her and they moved together until they cried out with each other's names on their lips. They held tightly to one another as the final moment of climax caught them up in its flood tide and swept them over the edge.

"I told you, my darling Mary Beth," Nick murmured long afterward, "you're perfect to kiss, perfect to touch, perfect to love."

"And I love loving you," she reciprocated, curling up into his side, happy, content, at peace with herself and the crazy world.

"I want us to get married just as soon as we can make the arrangements," Nick told her even later.

"Yes, we'll have a simple but elegant wedding here at the house," she suggested, rubbing her chin along his shoulder. "It will be my fond farewell to this place. Then it will be officially turned over to the Williams Library as my grandfather always intended it should be."

Nick watched her through the eyes of love. "Will you mind so very much?"

"What? Giving this place up?" Mary Beth gazed up into those eyes, nearly drowning in what she beheld there. "Not half as much as I'd thought. I'll have my memories, of course. But it's the future I'm interested in gambling on now."

Nick took her in his arms and rolled her over onto his stomach. "Gamble? What gamble? How can we lose when we'll have each other to bring us luck?"

She ran her hands lovingly over his chest and shoulders. "By the way, what will we tell people, in years to come, when they ask us how we met?"

"That's easy," Nick drawled lazily as he began to nibble her ear. "We'll tell them the truth. We'll tell them we were introduced by Lady Luck herself."

Take 4
Silhouette Special Edition novels
FREE...

and preview future books in your home for 15 days!

Start with 4 FREE books, yours to keep. Then, preview 6 brand-new Special Edition® novels—delivered right to your door every month—as soon as they are published.

When you decide to keep them, pay just $1.95 each ($2.50 each in Canada), *with no shipping, handling, or other additional charges of any kind!*

Romance *is* alive, well and flourishing in the moving love stories presented by Silhouette Special Edition. They'll awaken your desires, enliven your senses, and leave you tingling all over with excitement. In each romance-filled story you'll live and breathe the emotions of love and the satisfaction of romance triumphant.

You won't want to miss a single one of the heart-felt stories presented by Silhouette Special Edition; and when you take advantage of this special offer, you won't have to.

You'll also receive a FREE subscription to the Silhouette Books Newsletter as long as you remain a member. Each lively issue is filled with news on upcoming titles, interviews with your favorite authors, even their favorite recipes.

To become a home subscriber and receive your first 4 books FREE, fill out and mail the coupon today!

Silhouette Special Edition®

Silhouette Books, 120 Brighton Rd., P.O. Box 5084, Clifton, NJ 07015-5084

Silhouette Desire

COMING NEXT MONTH

OUT OF THIS WORLD—Janet Joyce
When Adrienne met Kendrick, she thought he was an alien from
outer space. He insisted he wasn't, but how could she believe him
when his mere touch sent her soaring to the heavens?

DESPERADO—Doreen Owens Malek
Half Seminole Indian, Andrew Fox had chosen the dangerous life
of a bounty hunter. As a student of Indian folklore, Cindy found
him fascinating—as a woman, she found him irresistible.

PICTURE OF LOVE—Robin Elliott
It didn't take Steve long to realize Jade was the woman for him, but
Jade was a compulsive overachiever. Could she manage to temper
her ambition and make room for love?

SONGBIRD—Syrie A. Astrahan
Desirée had to choose—her career as a disk jockey in California or
Kyle Harrison, the man she loved, in Seattle. Could she possibly
find the best of both worlds?

BODY AND SOUL—Jennifer Greene
Joel Brannigan fought for what he wanted, and he wanted
Dr. Claire Barrett. She was ready for a fair fight, but Joel didn't
fight fair...and he always won.

IN THE PALM OF HER HAND—Dixie Browning
Fate had thrown Shea Bellwood and Dave Pendleton together under
rather bizarre circumstances, but who can argue with fate—
especially when it leads to love.
